Lee and the Consul Mutants

Keith Charters

STRIDENT

www.stridentpublishing.co.uk

Published by
Strident Publishing Ltd
22 Strathwhillan Drive
East Kilbride
G75 8GT

Tel: +44 (0)1355 220588
info@stridentpublishing.co.uk
www.stridentpublishing.co.uk

....

Print history
First published in 2004 by Neil Wilson Publishing
under ISBN 1-903238-82-X
Reprinted 2005 by Neil Wilson Publishing
Reprinted 2006 by Strident Publishing Ltd
ISBN 978-1-905537-01-3

This edition 2010 by Strident Publishing Ltd

A catalogue record for this book is
available from the British Library.
ISBN 978-1-905537-24-2

Typeset in Gotham
Interior designed by Melvin Creative
Cover by Lawrence Mann
Printed by JF Print

Keith Charters

has lived all over the UK, and now lives near Glasgow. He studied at the University of Strathclyde and should have gained a first class honours degree, but missed out by half a percent, mainly because he was playing snooker when he should have been studying. (Let this be a lesson to all.)

After graduating, Keith worked in various business management roles, ending up in London, where he headed up part of a big, rather strange, financial company in which staff got paid for shouting at their customers ... and at each other. It was weird.

At this point Keith started writing a lot. An awful lot. Soon writing was taking over his life. So he took a deep breath, gave up his 'proper' job and began writing full-time.

Lee and the Consul Mutants was the first fruit of his labours. It took the no.1 spot in *The Herald's* Children's Bestsellers chart during 2006, with *Lee Goes For Gold* no.4 at the same time. Keith never looked back. Out came *Lee's Holiday Showdown* followed by *Lee on the Dark Side of the Moon* However, you can read the Lee novels in any order you like.

As well as writing, Keith now visits over 100 schools, libraries and book festivals each year and is renowned for his hilarious and energetic events. If you would like to invite Keith to visit your school, email him at:

keith@keithcharters.co.uk

This book is for:

Mel, Murray and Daniel

Chapter One

Lee's day was going downhill faster than a skier racing to escape an avalanche.

No sooner was he sitting at his desk than his teacher, The Ogre (also known as Mrs Ogilvy), was shouting at him. 'You've forgotten your homework *again*, Lee! Honestly, it's a wonder you remember to come to school in the mornings.'

Lee thought of what his dad sometimes said – about dogs' barks usually being worse than their bites. It clearly didn't apply to ogres, though; or certainly not to the one leaning over Lee, because it was her *breath* that was worse than her bite. *Much* worse. It was as if she'd eaten curry for breakfast and forgotten to clean her teeth.

'Come on, Ogre, it's tough for me. My parents are divorced and every day I've got to shift my few meagre belongings between two homes. Plus my granny's really sick and I have to help look after her. And on top of all that, I have to spend the evenings cleaning the house while my parents work in dead-end jobs just so we can afford to eat. Can you really blame me if I forget my homework once in a while? All that responsibility at my age … it's just not fair.

1

Something's bound to slip. I'm only human!'

What a great defence! A high-powered lawyer couldn't have done better.

Except that Lee hadn't spoken these words, just thought them. And a few minor details weren't quite accurate. Teency weency little details, such as ...

Well, for a start, his parents weren't actually divorced; indeed they were perfectly happily married, and so the only things he ever shifted between two houses were his computer games.

Also, Lee didn't have a sick granny. Both his grannies were as fit as fiddles, so much so that they were always trying to outdo each other with tales of their remarkable health. If they were to be believed (which they weren't) then each ought to own a collection of Olympic medals.

Nor did Lee's parents make him clean the house, because they both had good jobs and paid a cleaner to come round once a week while Lee was at school. ('It means we can spend quality time together when we're not at work,' his mum would remind his dad whenever he complained about the cost, which was often.)

No, sadly, forgetting his homework was entirely Lee's own fault. There was nothing for it but to grin and bear The Ogre venting her annoyance at his oversight.

Still, the good thing about having a bad start to the day is that things can only get better.

At least, that's the theory. However, Lee's day didn't think much of theories and was determined to get even worse.

After morning interval the class bustled down to the assembly hall for Music – a chance for Lee to put behind him the incident with The Ogre.

Lee liked Music, certainly more than long-winded Language, mind-numbing Maths or sleep-inducing Science. Lee didn't even mind that Music was taken by The Rat (aka Mr Barratt).

The Rat was a tall, thin man who, in certain respects, reminded Lee of his Uncle Raymond, although Uncle Raymond was a farmer and had a sound excuse for wearing dirty rags and stinking – an excuse The Rat didn't have.

The Rat's jacket (his *only* jacket as far as Lee could tell) was the colour of a fresh cowpat. It smelled like one, too, which explained why flies seemed to follow him wherever he went. His trousers, which might once have been light grey, were now a splodgy mix of colours, as if he'd squirted tomato sauce in the direction of his dinner and ended up with most of it on himself. (He must then have made the fatal mistake of not immediately soaking his trousers in lukewarm water, the way Lee's mum said you always ought to.) The Rat also always wore a green and red tartan tie – a scratchy woollen one that could be substituted for sandpaper if ever there was a shortage.

'Morning, Mr Barratt,' Lee said as he passed at a distance his nostrils considered safe.

The Rat looked up from his piano. 'Oh, morning, Lee.'

One of the reasons Lee liked Music was that sometimes at the end of the class, if they'd all sung particularly well, The Rat would entertain them with the sort of music he loved to play in his spare time. Boogie woogie, he called it. However, Lee's dad had some CDs of the same sort of music, and he called it honky tonk. Given how The Rat smelled, honky seemed so much more appropriate.

Whatever it was called, The Rat could play it brilliantly. His hands would leap over the piano keys like a barefooted man walking on hot coals, while everyone tapped their feet to the tremendous rhythm. (Whereas, in Maths or Language pupils only ever tapped their feet as a means of staying awake.)

However, on this day The Rat had an unpleasant surprise in store – an unpleasant surprise of the sort that made most of Lee's class wish The Rat would boogie woogie back down whichever honky tonk drain he'd climbed out of. Instead of singing *together*, like they always did, he wanted each of them to sing alone, *in front of the rest of the class!*

Aaagghhh!

Most of the class groaned, but of course, some were perfectly happy to sing solo for The Rat. Those like Soppy Sophie, who was always going on about how she was in love with this or that singer from a boy band she'd seen on TV; or like Cretinous Kevin who was a real show-off and, rather annoyingly, had a great voice to show off with.

The Rat seemed oblivious to the torture he was inflicting. 'Sing out! Sing out!' he taunted as each pupil's turn came around, 'Chin up, shoulders back,' he continued, circling like a vulture eyeing prey.

As Lee's turn drew closer it wasn't *singing* out he was thinking of, but *getting* out. The door was close, but not close enough for him to escape unnoticed. He'd have feigned losing his voice if he'd thought there was a chance of getting away with it, but The Rat would never believe Lee's voice had disappeared in the thirty minutes since he'd said hello.

Lee noticed the clock on the wall, and willed the hands forward. But they stuck stubbornly to their usual extra-slow schooltime pace and he eventually had to join The Rat at the front of the room.

Everyone who'd gone before him could now relax. They sniggered as Lee cleared his throat, preparing to make a fool of himself. He wasn't a great singer and had no ambition to appear on Top of the Pops, so why did he have to go through with this?

The Rat gave him an introductory note, then left Lee to do his worst. Lee raised his chin and put his shoulders back as instructed, but it made no difference. He cringed at the sounds that rose from his throat. He'd heard sick dogs at the vets howl more tunefully. His voice was all over the place, like an adventurer who'd lost his map. It was SO embarrassing!

After the emotional torture of Music, food was a mightily appealing prospect. Lunchtime was Lee's second favourite time of the day – second to 'going home' time, of course – so he charged down the corridor, hoping to be first in line at the canteen.

Lee didn't quite make it into first place, though. It was school policy that anyone with a broken limb was allowed to leave their classroom a few minutes early at lunchtime, with a classmate of their choice so they wouldn't be trampled in the stampede for the canteen. And, as usual, Angelina Bottle (not to be confused with her sister, Genie) was ahead of him.

There was always something wrong with Angelina, though never anything really serious, and Lee was quite convinced that she made up ailments just to get to the front of the queue.

'What's wrong with you this time?' Lee asked. 'Broken another fingernail?'

Just as she was about to come back with a witty retort, the shutters rose to reveal the food on offer, and Angelina's attention immediately turned towards the feast set out before her.

Lee was equally distracted by the greens and reds of the salads and yellows and oranges of the fruit bowls. All that healthy food was just waiting for ...

... someone else. Because Lee was only interested in the hot dogs. He'd had one every lunchtime for the last three years. These days the kitchen staff didn't even ask what he wanted; as soon as they saw him they reached for the tongs and lifted a long, thin sausage onto a roll, as if loading a torpedo into a submarine.

Lee grabbed a carton of milk and made for the seats,

looking out for his best friend, Will. He spotted him halfway down the line and waved, but when Will responded halfheartedly Lee shrugged and returned his attention to the hot dog before him.

Lee and Will enjoyed each other's company – which was just as well, because they rarely had anyone else's. They didn't get picked on at school, but neither were they invited to join in games in the playground. It was as if they could see each other but no-one else could see them.

Lee was generally happy having just one close friend because you could play most things with two people; like draughts, computer games and wars. But it did have its disadvantages, as Lee had discovered when Will had suffered from chickenpox. Will had been off school for two whole weeks and it had been terrible, not only for Will, with all his itchy spots, but for Lee as well. Until then he'd thought there was no limit to the amount of time you could spend alone playing computer games or watching TV, but that fortnight had taught him there was. He suddenly discovered what it meant to be lonely. Towards the end, things became so bad that he'd even thought about playing with his four-year-old sister, Rebecca, and her stupid dolls, though fortunately it hadn't quite come to that.

Will eventually collected his lunch and joined Lee, who

moved his jacket off the seat he'd been saving.

'How was Moany this morning?' Lee asked, referring to Miss Malone, Will's teacher.

'Fine,' Will replied without looking up.

Lee was immediately suspicious. 'Fine? Are you sure?' Moany was never fine. She was always either 'awful' or 'even worse than usual.'

'I suppose,' Will said.

Lee had a good look at Will, who still hadn't made eye contact and was prodding his baked potato without the usual enthusiasm. 'Did she shout at you?'

'No.'

'So what's wrong then?'

Lee thought Will was about to cry and wondered what terrible calamity had befallen him. Had his Granny finally popped her clogs? (She'd never been quite as fit as either of Lee's.) Had his hamster finally worked out that the wheel in his cage wouldn't take him anywhere and gone on hunger strike demanding better transport? Or had Will's mum accidentally used their secret stash of wooden spears as firewood?

Will finally raised his head. 'We might be moving,' he said.

Lee was surprised. 'Might we?'

'No, not *you!* Me and my family.'

'What ... *moving* moving?'

Will nodded unhappily.

'What's wrong with where you are?'

'Mum and Dad want a bigger house,' Will said.

'But what about school?' Lee asked, the terrible implications becoming clearer by the second.

'I'll probably end up having to go to another one.'

'No! You can't!'

'Mum and Dad say I might have to.'

'But ... when?'

'Whenever we move.'

This was bad. Really really bad. The kind of really bad that really ought not to get much worse.

Now Lee could understand why Will had lost his appetite, because he'd just lost his own.

All afternoon Lee thought about Will moving house. What would it mean to their friendship? What would it be like if each playtime and lunchtime Will wasn't there to talk to? And what would it be like trying to play wars on his own? (Boring – he would win all the time.) He thought about it all through Language and French and didn't even care when The Ogre shouted at him for not paying attention.

The bad-breathed old crone could holler all she wanted; it wasn't *her* life that was about to be ruined. *She* wasn't the one about to lose *her* best friend.

Lee hardly even noticed when the bell rang for the end of the day. Usually he leapt up with great enthusiasm and dashed for the door (more often than not forgetting to pack his homework into his schoolbag as he rushed to leave the classroom). But this time he rose slowly from his seat, thinking of how in the days and weeks ahead he would have to make the journey home on his own.

Will was waiting for him at the school gates, just as glum as at lunchtime.

'Couldn't you ask your mum and dad if you could stay with *us* until you finish school here?' Lee asked as they shuffled dejectedly through the school gates.

'I've already tried that one, but they said "no".'

'Well can't you say it'll have a terrible effect on your education if you change schools?'

'I've tried that, too.'

'Did you tell them you'll hate it at another school?'

Will nodded. 'Lee, I've tried *everything*, but nothing's worked.'

Lee suspected this meant Will might even have resort - ed to tears, but he didn't embarrass his friend by asking.

Chapter
Two

Lee awoke the next morning with a pain in his side. And for once it wasn't his little sister.

He'd had the pain since arriving home the previous afternoon but had ignored it, assuming its cause was Will's devastating news about moving house. However, the pain was still there now, and he felt really tired, too, the sort of tired you might just about recover from if you slept straight through until the following Christmas. He certainly didn't feel like going to school (even more so than usual), so when his mum came in to drag him out of bed he made no effort to hide his discomfort, groaning and wincing when she tried to move him.

Lee's mum eyed him up and put her hand on his forehead. He wondered what she thought that would tell her. It was hardly a scientific method for assessing illnesses. If that was all there was to being a nurse or doctor then how come they required years of training?

'Hmmm,' she said with a look Lee recognised as meaning she was trying to work out if he was genuinely ill or faking it. 'Well, I guess Dad had better call the doctor and work from home.'

He thought about telling her he wasn't *that* ill – that it would probably pass by the end of the day and certainly wasn't worth dragging the doctor out for because surely there were people far more ill than him who needed attention – but he was too tired to argue, so he said nothing and his mum went downstairs.

A minute later Lee's dad stepped into the bedroom doorway. 'Want a bacon sandwich for breakfast?' he asked brightly.

Lee loved bacon rolls, especially with half a bottle of tomato sauce on them, but he said, 'To be honest, Dad, I'm really not very hungry.'

'Hmmm.' His dad turned to Lee's mum, who'd joined him. 'Doesn't even fancy a bacon roll for breakfast. I guess that means he really *must* be ill.'

This struck Lee as no more scientific a method of assessing his health than his mother's hand-on-forehead routine, but again he didn't argue the point.

'Do you feel hot?' his mum asked.

'No,' Lee said.

'Do you feel cold?'

'No.'

'Itchy?'

'No.'

'Well how *do* you feel, then?' his dad asked, a little impatiently. 'Give us a clue!'

'My side's sore.'

'Like a stitch?'

'Sort of like one, but not really.'

That got another 'hmmm' from his parents, from which he deduced that he wasn't helping them much.

'Well it's sore like one, only it's not as sharp.'

'More a dull ache, then?' his dad enquired.

Lee couldn't think of a better way to describe it, so he nodded.

'That's all, though. You don't have any other aches or pains?'

Rebecca was at the childminders, so that pain had gone. 'No. I'm just tired.'

'Did you go straight to sleep last night or did you sit up reading?'

It was a fair enough question – Lee often sat up reading for ages and ages, but last night he hadn't. 'I went straight to sleep.'

'Are you sure?' his dad double-checked.

'I promise.'

Lee's dad sighed, finally convinced. 'Okay, I'll call the office and let them know I'm not coming in.'

Lee was woken by the sound of footsteps approaching his bed. He looked up and saw a tall, middle-aged man.

'Hi there, I'm Doctor Philadopolopolus.'

'Doctor who?'

'No, Doctor Philadopolopolus,' the man said, grinning at a very bad joke he obviously used several times a day. 'But call me Doctor P – it's easier to pronounce.'

Doctor P had with him a large black bag that looked alarmingly like a toolkit. Lee worried that it contained saws for performing emergency amputations of arms and legs when they couldn't get patients to hospital in time.

'What time is it?' Lee asked, rubbing his eyes but making no attempt to sit up.

'Twenty-five past two,' his dad told him.

'Aw,' Lee said, vaguely realising he'd been asleep for four or five extra hours.

'Right then, young man,' the doctor said, 'let's see if we can work out what's up with you.'

Doctor P placed a freezing hand on Lee's forehead. It made Lee jump, but he soon fell still again because moving so suddenly had hurt his side.

'Are you still tired?' Doctor P asked.

The very mention of tiredness brought on a yawn from Lee.

'I'll take that as a "yes",' Doctor P said. 'Now, Lee, if you'll just lift your pyjama top, I need to have a poke around your tummy. That's where it's hurting, isn't it?'

It was, and now that Lee was properly awake he realised it was hurting more than ever, so he lifted his top.

'Tell me if it's painful anywhere in particular when I press,' the doctor instructed, and he began prodding with his bony fingers.

'Aooh!' Lee cried, like a dog that's just had its paw trodden on.

'Sore there?' Doctor P asked.

Lee nodded rapidly. Of course it was sore!

The doctor continued prodding and it hurt every time he pressed Lee's right-hand side, just below his belly button.

'Okay,' Doctor P said, seemingly satisfied he'd found the cause of the trouble. He walked towards the door. 'Can I have a word?' he asked Lee's dad, who followed him out of the room.

Lee could hear a low mumble coming from the landing but couldn't make out what the two men were saying.

It was a couple of minutes before his dad led the doctor back into the room. They both looked serious. Had they phoned the school and spoken to the dinner ladies? Had those sweet old women spilled the beans and put him in soapy bubble? Had Doctor P somehow found out about all the hot dogs Lee had eaten for lunch over the last three years?

'Lee, you need to go to hospital,' Doctor P announced.

Lee stared up at his dad, suddenly wishing he'd agreed to eat the bacon roll at breakfast. 'Hospital! Why, what's wrong with me?'

'Well, I think there might be a problem with your appendix.'

'My appendix?' Lee was confused. 'Isn't that something at the back of a book?'

Doctor P leaned over. 'It's an organ,' he explained, 'just like your heart or your lungs, except that it doesn't actually do anything and so nobody really knows why we have one. However, sometimes it can burst and that can be very dangerous, so I'd like you to go in to hospital so the doctors there can check you out properly.'

'Aw,' Lee said, thinking that the appendix sounded like a stupid design fault. If God existed then he really ought to get some new technical staff. 'Can I go in on Thursday afternoon? I've got French then, and I hate it.'

'I was thinking of rather sooner than that,' Doctor P said

with a warm smile. 'I'll call an ambulance in a moment.'

'An ambulance! No way, José! They're for people who're dying. I've just got a slightly sore tummy.' He looked pleadingly at his dad. 'Listen, Dad, I was only kidding about being ill. I just wanted to be off school because I was really tired. You don't have to send me to hospital. I promise I'll go to school tomorrow and I'll even do extra homework to catch up.'

Lee's dad bent down beside him.

'Lee, you're tired because you're not well, and sleeping's your body's way of trying to fight this infection. I know you like the odd lie in, but you never sleep till this late.'

'But Dad, I don't want to go to hospital!'

'I could go with you,' his dad offered, turning to Doctor P to check that it was okay.

'I'm sure that would be fine,' Doctor P said.

Lee's dad turned back to Lee and smiled. 'Maybe they'll turn on the siren and all the traffic will have to dive out of our way.'

Lee suspected his dad harboured a secret desire to ride in an ambulance and was going to make the most of this, his big opportunity. He could imagine him behind the ambulance's mirrored windows, shouting at other drivers, 'Get out of the way, my son's coming through!' It would be humiliating. He was a grownup, not a kid playing at emergencies.

And then a thought occurred to Lee, which he voiced aloud. 'Can I go on a stretcher?'

'Do you want to?' Doctor P asked.

'Well ... '

The timing couldn't have been better.

'It's here!' Lee's dad called as the ambulance pulled up outside at precisely three o'clock. A minute later Lee's bedroom was occupied by his dad, Doctor P and two friendly paramedics (who, it turned out, weren't doctors who arrived by parachute, as Lee had always thought).

The paramedics were wearing exactly the same pale green uniforms Lee had seen on *Casualty*, one of his mum's favourite programmes. Maybe that meant there would be a film crew waiting to capture his arrival at the hospital, and perhaps next week, when his mum watched, she would see him being pushed in through the emergency doors on a trolley! Then he'd be able to tell everyone at school he'd been on TV, and that would be brilliant!

While he thought this, the paramedics rolled him up in a blanket and lifted him gently onto the stretcher they'd laid next to him on his bed. The blanket was tight around every part of him except his stomach and he imagined himself as a caterpillar wrapped in a cocoon, waiting to change into a butterfly.

If it was weird being carried from his bedroom in a horizontal position, it was plain scary being manoeuvred down the steep stairs to the front door. 'Watch out for the loose carpet halfway down!' he warned the paramedics, worried they'd trip and send him flying.

Lee had never paid any attention to the ceilings of his family's home. They really weren't that interesting. However, now he didn't have any choice, and noted that the one above the stairs could do with a fresh coat of paint, preferably in a colour other than the bright banana yellow his mum had chosen last time.

'What time is it?' Lee asked his dad again.

'Why are you so bothered about the time?'

'Just curious,' Lee replied, pretending it didn't matter.

His dad checked his watch. 'Coming up to ten past three.'

Lee allowed himself a slight pained grin as they reached the bottom step and his dad opened the front door.

Lying on his stretcher, Lee could see that a solitary fluffy cloud was temporarily shading the world outside. Soon the gentle breeze would carry it away and, for a few minutes, the sun would regain its strength.

But who cared about the weather when the world outside was full of schoolchildren desperate to know what was going on at Lee's house!

As his house was on the escape route from school, all the pupils had seen the ambulance park outside, and, figuring something exciting must be happening, had flocked to see what that something was.

Everyone has a moment of stardom in their life and Lee recognised this as his. When he was gone, everyone would miss him. Kids he lived beside; kids he occasionally walked to school with because they passed his door; kids he liked and kids he considered sworn enemies – all would remember this for the rest of their lives as *The Day They Took Lee To Hospital*.

Even kids who barely gave him a second glance (and that was most kids) would no longer say, 'Lee who?' or 'Lee … oh, that little squirt.' Instead they'd say, 'You mean *the* Lee, the one they had to take away in the ambulance because he was at death's door, ringing the bell to be let in?' or '*That* Lee – the one who bravely endured the terrible agonies of something going horribly wrong with his appendix. What a kid! What a hero! What I'd give to be like him!'

Yes, that was what they'd say. The nation would take him

to their heart. He'd be a role model for others and posters of him would hang on bedroom and classroom walls across the country. Printers would struggle to produce enough copies to satisfy demand, and the Queen might even write to ask for his autograph. Kids wouldn't even add the moustaches, beards and glasses that they drew onto every other picture of someone's head. He would be invited onto TV chat shows alongside footballers and pop stars, and sponsorship deals worth millions would follow. Yes, he would be a superstar.

Having convinced *himself* of all this, Lee decided he'd better convince the crowd that had gathered to see him make his momentous journey. He needed to appear worthy of the ambulance and of the siren that would surely sound as he was rushed off to hospital.

So he scrunched up his eyes to make it look as if he was in tortured agony but fighting it bravely. It helped that the sun came out and blinded him.

Heads appeared above him as the paramedics passed beyond the garden gate.

'What's wrong?' someone asked.

'Why's he going in the ambulance?' asked another, clearly impressed.

Maybe this called for a few words, Lee thought.

Hi, fans. Yes, I know you're sad to see me being carried away like this, but I'll be back shortly, never fear. Oh by the way, watch Casualty *on Friday night because I'll be on it ... No, no, I can't sign autographs now ... Not unless you've got a pen handy ...*

Then again, maybe it would be best to suffer in silence – to show that he wasn't making the most of it the way some footballers did when they were fouled. Maybe that was the way to win true respect.

'Is he going to hospital?' asked a young boy he couldn't see.

No, I'm going on my holidays you idiot! Lee wanted to call out. *That's why the big white taxi's here!*

The questions kept on coming and Lee was dimly aware of his dad trying to answer some of them.

More and more kids crowded round, trying to get a last look before Lee left them.

'How fast can the ambulance go?' the paramedics were quizzed.

'Which hospital are you taking him to?'

'Are they going to give him injections with huge big sharp needles and then slice him open with a ginormous sword ...?'

What! Lee immediately opened his eyes and tried to sit

up, but the blankets were too tight.

The young girl's voice continued. ' ... And then are they going to cut out all his insides like they did with William Wallace ...?'

The female paramedic put a hand on Lee's shoulder to keep him lying completely flat.

In any case it was too late. There was a bang as the doors of the ambulance closed behind him.

Chapter
Three

The hospital was a blur of nurses in blue uniforms and doctors in white coats. They asked Lee questions and prodded his tummy, just as Doctor P had done earlier. Lee again provided them with a yelp when they found the place that was sore.

Lee's dad sat on the edge of the bed and kept saying everything was alright, but Lee wasn't convinced. His dad had phoned his mum, who'd said she would get there 'as fast as possible'. That only made Lee more worried. Why would his mum be rushing to the hospital if everything was going to be alright? Surely the fact that she was busting a gut to get across town was a very strong indication that things were NOT alright, that they were VERY VERY WRONG.

Lee decided to go to sleep again. In truth, he didn't have much choice. He'd never felt so tired before, not even after he and Will had tried to stay awake all night on a sleepover.

When Lee awoke again his mum was at his bedside.

'Hi, Dear,' she said in a coogy coogy coo voice that made

Lee feel two years old.

He smiled, at the same time becoming aware that he was somewhere different from before. He turned his head so he could swivel his eyes and have a good look around.

He was on a long ward, with a row of ten beds on either side. So far as he could see, children occupied them all. At the far end of the ward a television hung from a bracket on the wall but was switched off. At the other end was a set of double doors.

'How are you feeling, Little Dumpling?' Lee's mum asked.

Lee liked dumpling, but as a food, not as a pet name. He knew she meant well, but did she have to call him those sorts of names with so many other people around? Parents could be so embarrassing sometimes.

So how *did* he feel? Still tired, he realised, despite having slept for ... well, long enough for them to have moved him onto this ward without him waking up, and long enough for his mum to have arrived from work.

'Where's Dad?'

'He's just gone to get some coffee.'

'Aw.'

An itch made itself known on Lee's nose and he went to scratch it, but his mum leapt forward like a goalkeeper saving a penalty. 'Careful!'

'What?' Lee asked, wondering what on earth she was in such a panic about. And then, peering down over his chest, he saw his arm. 'Aghhh! What's happened to me? What have they done!'

Something was attached to his arm, something from which a thin, clear plastic tube wound its way up to a pouch of fluid hanging from a metal frame that reminded Lee of a netball hoop.

What was this contraption? Was it designed to suck out all your life force so the hospital could sell it to aliens? Or was the fluid moving into his body, not out? Was it a drug to make him remember his homework more often? Had his teacher really been *that* frustrated by his forgetfulness?

Lee had a faint recollection of having been briefly roused by something sharp and painful earlier, but he'd drifted off back to sleep without opening his eyes. Now he understood! They'd been sticking a needle in his arm!

'Don't worry, Lambkin.' The names were getting worse. 'It's just a drip.'

Lee wasn't sure if she was referring to the contraption itself or some man who'd put it there.

'It pumps lots of really good things into your body,' his mother explained further.

Lee wondered how you could get bacon rolls and sweets

down a tube that narrow. The only thing that would fit down it would be the milk of human kindness, but he'd never seen that for sale in supermarkets.

'Why do I need it?' Lee asked, not at all keen on the idea of having something stuck into one of his arms on a long-term basis. He scratched his nose with his other hand, relieved to find that the arm it was attached to was a tube-free zone.

'Well, Pumpkin, the doctor thinks you need to have an operation ... '

Aghhh! An operation! What that girl had said before the ambulance doors had closed – about slicing him open and rearranging his internal organs – it was all true!

'No, Mum, that can't be right!' He made a big effort to sound convincing. 'Honestly, I just didn't want to go in to school today.'

'But you've slept for most of the day, Poppet.'

'But *you* sometimes lie in for ages at weekends,' Lee pointed out. 'And they're not giving you an operation, are they!'

Lee could hear his mum's next words even before she spoke them. 'But that's different,' she would say, because that was what adults always said if something was okay for them but not okay for children. It was a rubbish explanation, but one they used a lot.

'But that's different,' she said, right on cue.

'How?'

'Because that's just me recovering from working all week, and looking after you and Rebecca.'

'Well this is just me recovering from school!'

She shook her head. 'Didn't Dad and the doctor explain what's wrong with you?'

Now Lee thought about it, he recalled something about an organ exploding. He wished it had been the one in the church that he and his fellow pupils were dragged to at the end of each term, then they might not have to go again. Even French was better than having some minister droning on about how you ought to live your life.

However, Lee knew it wasn't that sort of organ that had gone bang. It was his appendix, as his mum was now explaining.

'They need to drain off the poison,' she said.

'Aw.' It seemed a reasonable explanation.

'You'll be fine, Little Bunny.' She rummaged in a bag. 'Look, I've brought your favourite pyjamas.'

He'd felt tired before, but the sight of the pyjamas his mum was holding brought him round more quickly than when he made for the school canteen at lunchtime.

'Mum, they're *not* my favourites! I hate those ones. Auntie Lorna gave me them for Christmas years ago and they're dreadful. They've got teddy bears on them! And they go so far up my legs I've had to tell Will they're shorts.'

'Oh, I thought you liked them.'

'No way! I only wear them because you keep putting them under my pillow.'

It was his mum's turn to say 'Aw'. She put the pyjamas back in the bag that lay in front of a locker at the side of Lee's bed.

'Talking of Will,' she said, 'I'll call him and see if he wants to come in and visit you.'

'Is it worth it?'

'Why, don't you want him to?'

'Yeah, if he wants. But I'll see him when I get home.'

'Right,' his mum said in a way that convinced Lee she meant the opposite.

'What is it?' he asked.

'Well you might be here for quite a while.'

'How long? Until tomorrow morning?'

'A bit longer than that, they seem to think.'

'How long then?'

Lee saw his mum's gaze drop for a second and knew instantly that bad news was coming his way. He felt like a turkey on the 24th of November being told Christmas was being brought forward a month.

'Well these things don't happen overnight, and you'll need a bit of time to recover … '

She was waffling and avoiding the subject, so Lee interrupted her. 'Mum, just tell me how long.'

'Probably about a week.'

A week! Lee tried to ignore all the exclamation marks that were charging around in his head, suddenly remembering that he was supposed to be *Lee The Brave*. Kids out there were assuming he was taking this in his stride. They had admired his courage in the face of adversity as he'd been carried out to the ambulance, and some of them had probably bought autograph books by now that he'd have to sign when he got out.

Even his mum was looking to see how he'd take this news and he didn't want her to worry about him.

'Eh, right. A week, then. Eh, well tell Will I'd love to see him just as soon as possible.'

In the years that followed, Lee would tell his friends (indeed anyone who would listen) that the next thing he remembered was being wheeled down the corridor on the way to the theatre.

He perked up at being told that was where he was going. He needed some cheering up after hours spent lying in bed, mostly snoozing, but otherwise staring at the ceiling checking for any spiders that could fall into his mouth if he kept it open while sleeping. Theatre sounded much more interesting. He hadn't realised they laid on those sorts of treats for kids in hospital. What would be on, he wondered. A comedy? A mystery? Even one of those daft sing-alongs would be okay compared to lying around all day in the ward, unable to move in case his drip became detached.

And would he be allowed an ice cream if there was an interval? He hadn't been allowed food for three days while the drip thing was stuck in his arm. He wasn't actually hungry, but you didn't need to be hungry to fancy an ice cream.

People stared down at him as he was wheeled up the corridor. Not just the nursing staff but other patients, many of whom were wandering around in their pyjamas. Had news of his illness spread far and wide? Were some kids faking illness just to get into hospital to catch a glimpse of him on a stretcher trolley? Would those same kids make miraculous recoveries later that same day and be out by dinnertime?

Trundling along the corridor, Lee reflected on how his whole world had changed over the last three days. He no longer saw everything from an upright position, but instead viewed it lying flat. Ceilings were like walls to him (except that it was difficult to hang pictures from them) and walls were like floors (you had to be careful not to fall down through all the doors). As for the floor ... well it was always behind him nowadays so he didn't have to worry about it.

Of course, what Lee wouldn't say in years to come was that the theatre he was being pushed to wasn't one that provided a little light relief for those stuck in hospital. It was the operating theatre. And as his trolley was rolled smoothly between the theatre's double doors, it was fear that was dribbling down his chin, not melting ice cream.

Looking around, it seemed as though the operating theatre was the venue for a fancy dress party to which everyone had turned up wearing long green gowns. Some also wore big plastic aprons, like the chefs on TV. He presumed they weren't there to make his lunch (it seemed rather unlikely they'd go to so much trouble, even for a celebrity like himself). And anyway, all you needed to make hot dogs was a microwave.

So what were they all there for?

Lee was hit by the frightening realisation that they might be about to cook him! They certainly looked weird enough to be into that sort of thing.

He desperately looked around for a large cauldron, but couldn't see one.

No, no, that couldn't be it. He reminded himself that he was a patient in a hospital, not the honoured guest of a witches' coven. They were going to operate, not make dinner out of him, though both involved a certain amount of carving.

He tried to see past all the bodies crowded around him. Were there any of the 'big sharp needles' or 'ginormous knives like swords' that the girl outside the ambulance had asked about?

One of the gowns bent over him. 'Okay now, Lee,' said a male voice from behind a white mask. (Did he not want Lee to recognise him afterwards? If so, why?) 'I'm going to give you a small injection to help you sleep, and then when you wake up, you'll be as right as rain.'

As right as rain? Lee thought. Wasn't that a contradiction? When it rained you got wet. When it rained your parents either made you play indoors or forced you to wear 'appropriate clothing', usually meaning a hideous bright orange cagoule that everyone would laugh at.

But now wasn't the time to debate the finer points of the English language, not when someone was reaching for something to stick in your arm, though first they were rubbing something on it and then lightly tapping the same spot and ... ouch! That would be the needle, then!

'Lee, I want you to count to ten for me. Can you do that?'

I can count to a million zillion gillion if you give me long enough, Lee wanted to say, but instead he did as the man asked. 'One, two ... three ... four ... f ... zzzzzzzzzzzzzzzzzzzzzzzzzzz ... '

Chapter Four

■ ■ ■ a zillion!

The first thing Lee noticed when he awoke was that his mum and dad were alongside his bed.

The second thing he noticed was the large tube sticking out of his side.

Aaaggghhhh!

He quickly closed his eyes again. He'd woken up too early, he decided. He was only at one zillion – there was still quite a way to go to reach a million zillion gillion. He'd best go back to sleep.

But his mum wasn't going to let him.

'Hi, Honeykins,' she purred like one of those friendly cats that follows you up and down the street rubbing itself against your legs.

'Welcome back, kiddo,' his dad said as if Lee had just landed back on Earth after being the first kid in space. 'How are you feeling?'

Lee had learned quite a few words in the playground that would adequately describe how he felt at this moment, but he didn't think his parents would appreciate him uttering any of them. In any case, he wasn't sure how he felt yet.

'What's happened to me?' he asked instead. 'Is that tube going to be there for the rest of my life?' He had visions of himself walking down the street and everyone pointing, saying, 'Hey, look, it's Tube Boy!'

'No, no,' his dad assured him. 'It's just so they can drain away the poison, like Mum told you before.'

'Aw.'

'But you mustn't turn over onto your front,' his mum said.

Lee looked down the bed to make certain they hadn't tied or chained him to it.

A nurse joined them.

'Hi, Lee,' she said. 'How are you feeling?' (He suspected this was a question he was going to be asked a thousand times over.)

'Alright.'

'You'll need plenty of rest.'

He was hardly in a fit state to get up and run around the ward! Lee could see that the tube ran out his side and continued on until it reached a sort of bag at the side of his bed. It was where all the poison was gathering. Uggh!

Rest. Right ... Hang on, wasn't that *all* he'd done for the last two or three days?

'Let me know if you need one of these,' the nurse said,

holding up a silver pan.

Bizarre! First they said he needed some rest, then they offered him the chance to do some cooking!

'I don't know any recipes,' Lee said, looking to his mum in the hope that she might be able to provide some.

His dad sniggered. 'Good to see you haven't lost your sense of humour, son.'

What was so funny? His mum's cooking wasn't *that* bad.

Lee dozed off again soon afterwards. When he awoke he had a different visitor hovering over him – a girl with long hair and a narrow face. Lee guessed she was about ten. He imagined his dad making one of his corny jokes about the nurses looking so much younger these days.

'You should be in the *Guinness Book of Records*,' she said in a bright voice.

'What?' Lee responded.

'You've slept for about a week.'

'A week! Great, does that mean I can go home now?'

'Well, maybe not quite that long, then, but ages and ages.' She adjusted a band in her hair, as if waiting for Lee to say something else. 'I'm Kate,' she said when he didn't. 'My bed's next to yours.'

Lee had wondered what was next to his bed. A green curtain had meant he hadn't been able to see anything in that direction.

A nurse smiled at them both as she passed the end of the bed.

'That's Kerry,' Kate said. 'Nurse Chicken.'

'Chicken ...?'

'Yes, I know it's a stupid name, but she's really nice.'

'Right ... ' Lee said.

'She fancies Mac,' Kate revealed, speaking quietly in case anyone other than Lee could hear her passing the secret. 'Doctor Donald's his proper name, but Mac's what she calls him when she thinks no-one's listening.'

'Aw,' Lee said again, disinterested.

'You can tell from the way she looks at him ... '

'Aw.' Lee tried to work out what day it was, what time it was and what would be on TV at that moment.

' ... I've seen him, too, and he's got lovely eyes ... ' Kate droned on while Lee wondered how he could get to the TV when there were so many tubes sticking out of him.

'I think mutants are trying to take over the hospital,' Kate said.

Maybe Lee could ask a nurse to move him ...

HANG ON! Lee slammed into reverse and tuned back in

to her conversation. 'What did you say?' he asked urgently.

'That Doctor Donald's got lovely eyes ...?'

'No, no, not that! About the mutants!'

'Oh, right. Well, I think they're trying to take over the hospital.'

'Why? And how are they doing it?'

Kate looked around, but there was no-one nearby. 'They're doing it by taking over the minds of some of the staff,' she whispered.

'Really?'

'Look!' Kate didn't point but turned her head towards the double doors at the end of the ward. A man in a white coat had just passed between them. He was broad-shouldered and very tall, and his skin was light brown. As he walked, his body seemed to be slightly ahead of his limbs, as if his arms and legs were a little loose at the joints.

'Is he one of them?' Lee asked quietly, in case they had more sensitive hearing than human beings, more sensitive even than his dad's when he sneaked through to the lounge on Sunday mornings to watch TV before anyone else woke up.

Kate nodded. 'They never smile.'

Right enough, the tall man, who might otherwise have passed for a doctor, seemed worried that if he moved any part of his face his mask might crack and give him away.

'Who is he?' Lee asked, still whispering.

'His name is Doctor Enleader. But more important is *what* he is,' Kate said. (Lee would have told her to skip the grammar lesson if she hadn't possessed such crucial information.) 'I heard Nurse Chicken say he's a Consul Mutant.'

'Mutants that can change their shape to look like doctors! Wow! Cool!'

'I think they must use mind drugs, because they've got everyone else under their control. Whatever they say, the other staff do. Even the normal doctors.'

'How many mutants are there?' Lee pressed, anxious to know the size of the enemy force.

'Not many.'

'They must be really powerful, then,' Lee observed. 'Does anyone else know about them?'

'Carrie – the girl at the other end of the ward – she knows, but she's going home tomorrow.'

'Any boys?' Lee asked hopefully.

'I think Carrie's told Jason.'

'Good.' Lee's strategic mind, honed by games of chess, was already working overtime. 'We should tell all the other kids. We don't stand a chance on our own.'

'Stand a chance of what?'

'Of defeating them! What else!' That was the problem with girls. The military part of their brains wasn't as well developed because they didn't play wars, so when it came to saving the human race from evil alien invaders like the Consul Mutants they would always be one step behind.

'And I suppose you want *me* to relay the information to them,' Kate said, 'while *you* wait at headquarters and work out the strategy.'

'Well, I can't really ...'

'Move? No, you *can't*, can you.' And it seemed as if Kate wasn't going anywhere fast either. 'I'm not just going to be the messenger girl,' she said. '*I* told you about them, and *I'm* the one who understands the way they work, so if we're going to fight them *I* want to do a lot more than run from bed to bed passing on *your* messages. I'm not a carrier pigeon, you know.'

That was the other problem with girls; they were always demanding equal rights.

'How many of the kids here are mobile?'

Kate stood back from Lee's bed so she could see up the centre of the ward. 'Not many,' she said after counting. 'Most are in bed.'

'How come you're not?'

'Because I don't need to be,' she said.

'Why, what's wrong with you?'

'I've had an operation on my heart,' she said.

'What kind of operation?' Lee asked sensibly, knowing hearts were a serious business.

'They needed to replace a valve that wasn't working properly.'

'A valve? Like on a tyre.'

'Sort of. It's to make sure the blood only travels one way.'

'And is it all right now?'

Kate nodded.

'So how come you're still in hospital?' She appeared to Lee to be fine.

'They need to make sure everything's working properly.'

'Aw.'

Kate's face had gone red, so he left it at that.

'A couple of the others can get around in wheelchairs,' Kate offered, changing back to the original subject of their conversation. 'If there's someone around to push them, that is.'

Lee thought for a second. (He was a very quick thinker.)

'Well it sounds as if the enemy's men are extremely intelligent and powerful,' Lee said.

'So are their women,' Kate added.

'Right,' Lee conceded. 'So we'll need to be cunning if

we're going to defeat them. We need to think of a plan.'

Kate suddenly jumped away from the bed. Lee assumed she'd seen a Consul Mutant coming, and decided his own best course of action – given his inability to go anywhere at all – was to pretend he was sleeping again. He immediately closed his eyes tightly enough to convince any passer-by, but left them open just enough to ensure he could still see a blurred outline of everything around him. Had they been seen by the Consul Mutant who'd passed through the ward a short time ago? And had he told his commander that he'd seen two rebels discussing the overthrow of the Consul empire?

No. Through the slits of his eyes he saw Kate throw her arms around a woman who'd entered the ward, a woman whom he took to be her mum.

Lee opened his eyes properly again, the feared emergency over.

He'd learned important information from Kate – information that could be crucial to the survival of mankind. Now that she was gone he had time to think. And thinking was best done with your eyes closed, so he closed them again. And fell asleep.

Lee dreamed of how useful Will would be to the fight against the Consul Mutants if only he were in hospital with him.

Will was a scientific genius. He could make Lego missiles that exploded when they landed and that had their own missile launchers. He knew how to work a computer and get into all sorts of websites. And he knew which chemicals you needed to mix to make stink bombs so lethal they smelled like you'd just eaten a whole field of cabbages before dropping a humdinger.

But most importantly in Lee's current situation, Will was an *undiscovered* scientific genius. The Consul Mutants would never have heard of him, so if Lee could somehow get him into hospital he would be able to help in the fight against the intergalactic tyrants in white coats. He could hack into their computers to discover their weaknesses, then build a weapon to destroy them. Meanwhile, Lee would be able to think of a brilliant plan for an ambush. And maybe Kate would also have some ideas, too – despite being a girl.

One minute he was dreaming about Will, the next Will was there, right in front of him, at the end of his bed.

Spooky!

But was it Will? Or was this a shape-changing Mutant trying to fool him into giving himself away? Lee decided he would have to be careful. 'What's your name?' he asked.

'What? Lee, it's *me*!' Will said.

'Are you here on your own?' Lee asked, folding his pillow in two so he could use it to prop up his head.

'No, your mum and dad brought me.'

Lee looked around.

'Where are they then?'

'Your dad's gone to the toilet and your mum's gone to get something to drink. You were sleeping when we arrived.'

'Hmm,' Lee mused before realising that was the same sound his parents always made when they were unconvinced. It was too convenient; his parents away and, just at the moment Lee awakened, Will there on his own. Some more questions were required to check this person's true identity. Difficult questions. Questions to which only the real Will would know the answers.

'Who's Snotty?' he asked.

Will ran a finger across his nose, then peered at the results. 'There's nothing there,' he said.

'No, no, I don't mean you. I mean who's *called* Snotty?'

'Oh, right, you mean Mrs Snodgrass,' Will said. 'I thought you meant I had a bogey hanging out my nose.'

So the person (or thing) claiming to be Will knew who Snotty Snodgrass was. (She was the headmistress at their school. With a name like Snodgrass she hardly needed a nickname like the other teachers, but they'd given her one anyway – as an act of kindness given her real name.)

Will walked up the side of the bed as Lee said, 'Where's our secret stash of swordsticks?'

Will raised a hand and scratched his head.

Aha, Lee thought. Caught him out! So he is one of them!

But Will said, 'At the bottom of my garden, at the side of the old shed.' Will moved alongside the bed until he was level with Lee's head. 'But why are you asking me these things? Are you worried your memory might have been affected by the operation?'

Now Lee was convinced, because he was absolutely certain no one else knew where their swordstick stash was. It had to be the real Will.

'I thought you might be one of the aliens,' Lee told him. 'I had to check.'

'Eh ... oh, right. Lee, you should get some rest. I think this operation's made you go bonkers. Those painkilling drugs they're giving you must be really strong to affect your imagination like that.'

'No, no,' Lee insisted. 'They're Consul Mutants. The girl in the next bed told me. We've got to be careful in case they find out we know about them.'

Will peeked around the curtain that still ran up one side of Lee's bed. 'Lee, there's no-one in the next bed.'

'What! Oh no, they must have found out and taken her away!'

At that moment Doctor Enleader, the Consul Mutant Kate had pointed out before, strode past them in his gangly way, up the middle of the ward. As soon as he was out of earshot Lee beckoned Will closer. 'That was one of them,' he said. 'He might even be the head one, it's difficult to tell. They obviously don't wear badges to show their rank when they're disguised as humans.'

Lee told Will the rest of what he knew about the Mutants – how they controlled all the other staff, how they put tubes into you that sucked out your life force, and how they gave you injections to keep you in your bed so you wouldn't escape. Will appeared sceptical at first, but Lee could see his look change as he told him more of the worrying details.

'So it looks as if it might be down to you and me to save the world,' Lee concluded just at the moment his dad walked back through the double doors.

'Remember,' Lee said quickly to Will, 'parents can't tell the Mutants from other doctors, so don't tell Mum and Dad what I've told you.'

This would be their secret, just as it was a secret that Lee occasionally copied his homework from Will; or just as it was still a secret that the two of them had once discovered Will's mum's emergency supply of chocolate in the cupboard under the stairs and that, after scoffing the whole lot, they had punctured and shredded the wrappers with the pointed end of a compass to make it look as if a family of mice had been responsible. (Will's dad had laid a trap but, not surprisingly, had never caught anything.)

Will nodded.

'Kate.'

'What?'

'What happened to you?'

'What do you mean?'

'Earlier. Did they take you to their spaceship? I asked my friend Will to check you were okay, but when he pulled back the curtain you'd gone. I was worried in case they'd found out you knew about them.'

'I was in another part of the hospital for some tests,' Kate said as if it were no big deal.

'Hmm. Well anyway, can you let everyone know there'll be a Council of War at my bed as soon as the Mutants have checked up on everyone this afternoon?'

'A Council of War?'

'Yeah, to work out how to get rid of them.'

'Eh ... right. Who do you want me to invite?'

'All the kids on the ward.'

'But they won't all be able to make it.'

'Well all those who can, then. We can let the others know what we decide so they can help too.'

'Well, okay. I'll tell as many as I can. But won't it look a bit obvious if we all gather round your bed? Won't the nurses break up our meeting?'

Lee thought about this. Maybe Kate had a point.

'Maybe we should stick to two or three of us,' he said.

Kate agreed and set off to choose a few suitable can - didates, leaving Lee to mull over a plan.

'Morning, young Lee,' the woman with the breakfast trolley called.

Lee peered over his blankets. 'Oh. Morning, Isa.'

It was Lee's understanding that you were supposed to retire when you were sixty-five, but they'd obviously made an exception for Isa, because she had to be well over a hundred and twenty. Lee thought she ought to have an apostrophe in her first name – I'sa – then she could have a description for her surname. *I'sa very-old-lady-with-skin-more-crinkly-than-an-ancient-treasure-map*. Never mind double-barreled surnames, Isa's would be twelve-barreled. Mind you, no-one would ever write to her if she had a name that long.

Isa came round every morning at eight o'clock and, because there was so little to do if you were laid up in bed, her visits were one of the highlights of the day.

At first Lee had been impressed that Isa could remember everyone's name *(I'sa memory woman)*. That was, until he realised everyone had a name plaque at the end of their bed *(I'sa cheat)*.

Today was momentous. He was finally being allowed real

food again.

'First day of the rest of your life,' Isa told him. 'So, what's it to be?' she asked. 'Mind you've to build yourself up. Doctor's orders after all that time on your drip, Lee.'

'Can I have a bowl of Rice Krispies?'

'You can have whatever you want, young man,' she said, lifting up the packet and pouring him a bowl.

'There you go. That'll do you for starters. Let me know if you want some more.'

'Thanks, I'sa really hungry,' he said without thinking, but it was okay, Isa didn't seem to get it.

Lee wasn't just really hungry, he was absolutely ravenously starving, so much so that he was thinking of changing his name to Marvin – Starvin' Marvin. It had been ... well, how long had it been since he'd last taken food through his mouth instead of having stuff pumped into him through a drip? Four days? Five? A sign reading *Nil By Mouth* had hung above his bed throughout that time. Now, looking up, he could see that it was gone. He decided it meant he was on the mend.

He tore into his cereal. The little pieces of crisped rice whispered to him as he ate, repeating the same thing over and over again. *Snap, Crackle, Pop* they seemed to be saying. Or was it *Snap Crack Pots?* Or even *Zap Crack Pots!*

Maybe it was a warning about the crackpot Consul Mutants! Maybe even the cereal knew what was going on! But as Lee wasn't fluent in Rice Krispie he couldn't be certain.

In under a minute his bowl was empty.

Isa saw him as she crossed the ward. 'You finished that lot already, young man?' Lee nodded. 'Want some more then?' she offered.

Lee didn't have to be asked twice. (He didn't even have to be asked once because he would have asked Isa for some more even if she hadn't offered.)

His second bowl lasted about the same time as his first – not very long. Again Isa noticed as she zigzagged down the ward, and again she offered him some more.

And so it went on. Lee consumed bowl after bowl after bowl until finally, when he saw Isa heading his way yet again, he thought, *I'sa gonna puke*.

It was time to stop. (Hopefully it wasn't already too late.)

Isa shook her head as she pulled up at his bedside. 'Seven bowls! Well, I think that beats the previous champion. I'll write it down in my diary when I get home tonight, just in case you ever need proof to send to the *Guinness Book of Records*. You could be *The Boy Who Ate The Most Cereal In One Breakfast*.'

Lee thought that sounded cool. If he hadn't felt so full he might have asked if there was also a category for bacon roll eating. He reckoned he could do pretty well at that, too.

Isa laughed as she pushed her trolley towards the door. 'I'sa thinking you're going to be a big fat porker if you carry on eating that much every day,' she called over her shoulder to Lee.

Just when he was supposed to be getting better, Lee started feeling worse again. His chest felt tight, as if he had a terrible cold, and he started coughing a lot.

'Probably side effects of the anaesthetic,' Nurse Chicken told him. 'It's quite common. But I've asked Doctor Donald to take a look at you nonetheless.' Any excuse to have her beloved doctor on the ward with her, Lee thought.

Doctor Donald arrived a little later and poked about around the place where the tubes entered Lee's tummy. (Lee closed his eyes for that; it was one thing being able to see the dressing that covered the wound where the tube went in, it would be quite another seeing inside yourself. Uggh!) Then the doctor placed the cold end of his stethoscope on Lee's chest.

'Hmmm,' Doctor Donald said after a while, and Lee knew from past experience that 'hmmm' was rarely good.

'We'll book you in for an ultrasound,' Doctor Donald said, supposedly to Lee though it seemed he was really talking to Nurse Chicken and another doctor standing alongside him.

Ultrasound, Lee lay thinking after the doctor had gone. That didn't sound so bad. Presumably it was some kind of music therapy. He wished he'd brought his favourite CDs to play on whatever mega system they were planning to hook him up to.

A couple of hours later Lee found himself once again being wheeled down a corridor and into a room. This one was not much bigger than a school locker. Crushed into the room with him were Doctor Donald and a woman he hadn't met before whose hair was so long and curly she could easily have stored a packed lunch in it and no-one would ever have known. Lee was convinced it was a wig and kept looking for real hair underneath it.

'Right, Lee,' she said. 'I'm Veri, and this ... ' she pointed to her side ' ... is Fred.'

Lee rubbed his eyes with the hand that didn't have anything sticking out of it. Nope, even with his eyes rubbed he couldn't see anyone there, not even a very small man standing behind the screen. Which meant ... Veri thought the machine was a person!

Of course, maybe it was. Lee had heard about artificial intelligence, it was in lots of kids' programmes, so maybe they had it in hospitals. After all, he'd seen a lot of other hi-tech equipment there. Then again, she might be taking mind-bending drugs like the ones the police officer had taught his class about at school, and maybe Veri's surname was Scarywoman.

'What Fred does is look inside you to see what's going on.'

Lee took a good look at Fred. He (or it) looked like a computer, but instead of a normal screen he had what looked like a submarine's radar. He certainly bore no resemblance to any music system Lee had ever seen. A flex ran from Fred to something Veri was holding. It was about the size of a telephone handset and had to be Fred's hand.

'Fred looks inside me?' Lee queried. It wasn't so much the looking Lee was concerned about, it was how Fred was going to get inside him in the first place. There weren't many holes in his body and he was absolutely certain none were big enough for Fred to get through. This had to be some form of alien torture.

For a moment Lee forgot about the big tube sticking out of his side and checked to see if he'd be able to make the door without the doctors stopping him.

'We normally use Fred for looking at babies while they're still inside their mummy's tummies,' the mad Veri said.

Lee was none the wiser but said, 'oh right' as if he knew exactly what the crazy woman was talking about. There was no point in looking foolish without good reason. That was the job of politicians and the royal family.

'Now then,' Veri continued, apparently oblivious to Lee's concerns, 'all I have to do is put some jelly on your belly, then we can check you out on the telly ...' Lee felt sorry for whoever was going to get it with their ice cream that evening. Veri's hands were already covered by rubber gloves like the ones Lee's mum used when she did the washing up.

'This might feel a bit cold at first,' Veri warned, squeezing a big dollop of jelly out of a tube and onto Lee's belly.

Cold! Polar bears could get frostbite from that stuff!

Or so it seemed at first. It soon warmed up as Lee's body heat kicked in.

Once Veri was happy the jelly had been sufficiently well spread, she stretched Fred's arm until his hand could reach Lee's tummy. Doctor Donald stepped closer as Lee felt the hand slide over the jelly.

'There,' Veri said to Lee. 'You can see inside yourself.'

Seeing his guts wasn't in Lee's top ten things to do in life, but he nonetheless turned his head towards the radar screen. Maybe he'd be able to spot a few hot dogs; there had to be loads of them still in there, not to mention a whole box of Rice Krispies.

However, the quality of the picture was so poor it was impossible to distinguish anything. Those were his insides? They looked more like a swirling tornado. Where were all those organs he'd learned about in school – heart, lungs, kidneys …

'You have to know what you're looking for,' Veri admitted, moving Fred's hand around. 'Look, here.' She pointed at a shape in the centre of the picture, then hit a button on Fred's keyboard so that the shape suddenly became much bigger. 'That's your tube.'

So it was! Exactly the right cylindrical shape.

'What we're really looking for, though,' said Doctor Donald, ' is something less obvious – something that might be making you feel unwell still.'

Did he mean apart from the seven bowls of Rice Krispies, or had Isa kept her mouth closed (in a way that maybe Lee should have after his second or third bowl)?

'What sort of thing?' Lee asked. Surely he'd have noticed if something had climbed inside him.

'Fluid, for instance.'

Lee looked at the screen again. As far as he could make out there was already plenty of fluid sloshing around his insides.

'Now then, what's that?' Doctor Donald said as Fred's hand picked up a small white area. 'Can we have a closer look just there?' he asked Veri, pointing to it.

Veri twiddled some knobs to magnify the image. It still didn't look like anything in particular to Lee but Doctor Donald seemed to think he was onto something. 'Hmm,' he said, then 'Hmm, hmm'. That got Lee worried. If one hmm was bad, three had to be really really bad. And that wasn't good (obviously). It might even be the sort of really really bad that meant you got to sit in your very own wooden box and admire your very own flower bed – from six feet under.

Lee knew what a will was but had never before thought about writing one. Now he tried to write it in his head in case he didn't have much time left.

I, Lee, want my worldly possessions to be distributed thus:

To Will (appropriately enough), my bestest friend in the whole wide world, I leave: my collection of swordsticks; the insects we caught that are still in the jar at the back of the shed unless Dad's found them (oh, except that now I think of it they've probably all suffocated because I didn't put any holes in the lid or give them anything to eat, so maybe Will won't want a jar of dead things); my bike (though I'm not sure how he'll ride it at the same time as his own); my CDs (because he hasn't got very good taste in music, so this way I can help him improve it); and all my board games, even the ones with the pieces missing, which to be honest is most of them.

To my little sister, who can be a right pain in the backside sometimes, I leave my Thomas The Tank Engine and Postman Pat videos because they're really not very interesting now I'm older, whereas she likes that sort of thing. She can also have that book on horses that Aunt Janice got me a few Christmas's ago. It's dead boring – I think she must have given me it by mistake – and anyway girls like horsey things, which is why a lot look like them.

To the Cat & Dog Home I leave the lead I found that

didn't have a dog attached. Maybe the dog had been fat but went on a diet and lost so much weight it was able to slide out of the lead and gain its freedom. If so, good; though I hope it knew how to find its way home for its dinner. If not, it'll probably end up in the Cat & Dog Home, too, in which case it might get its old lead back. That's if they haven't put the dog down, of course …

Doctor Donald interrupted Lee's thoughts. 'Yep, I'm fairly certain that's the source of the problem.'

It was hardly an impressive army that arrived at Lee's bedside later that day for the Council of War. In addition to Kate there were two boys. One rolled up in a wheelchair that he was having difficulty propelling, while the other hobbled up to them on crutches he clearly hadn't got the hang of.

Lee surveyed his troops and wondered if it might not be better to simply accept the rule of the Consul Mutants rather than engage them in battle with such a puny force. But small armies had defeated big armies before, he reminded himself. All it took was firm leadership and a superior strategy. It was just a pity he couldn't see where either might come from.

The boy in the wheelchair introduced himself as Scott – or 'Scott with two "t"s' as he put it. (That was all they needed, someone obsessed with spelling.) Scott was big boned with a podgy face, but his most noticeable feature was, without a doubt, his hair. When it had last been cut someone – presumably his mum or dad – had obviously taken a soup bowl, stuck it over his head and then cut round it, because he looked like a monk.

By contrast, Andrew was so skinny he could have hidden behind a garden rake. He was tall, too, and reminded Lee of a stork, especially given the way he balanced on one leg.

'What are you in hospital for?' Lee asked Scott, resisting the temptation to suggest it might be for a hair transplant.

'An operation on my bowel.'

Lee wondered if this was the same item of crockery used for Scott's haircut.

'You mean the bit you store your jobbies in before you go for a poo?' Andrew said.

'Eh ... yeah ... '

'Yuck!' Lee exclaimed. 'Imagine being the surgeon who had to rummage around in there!'

Andrew giggled. 'I'll bet his family don't look forward to

him getting home at night.'

'Yeah, and I'll bet they make sure *he* washes his hands before dinner,' Lee said.

Kate looked at them both disapprovingly. 'That's not very nice.'

'Aw,' Lee said, realising he'd embarrassed Scott. 'Sorry.'

Andrew apologised too.

'It's alright,' Scott said. 'So what are you in for?' he asked Lee. 'How come you're stuck in bed?'

'These,' Lee told him, showing off his tubes.

'Wow!' Andrew said.

'Man!' Scott exclaimed.

'Gross,' Kate complained. 'Looking at them makes me feel ill.'

'So how come you've got them?' Scott pressed.

'My appendix exploded.'

'What's your appendix?' the other three asked, all at the same time.

Lee told them what Doctor P had told him back at the house.

'So one minute you were sitting there, the next ... Boom! as if someone had planted a bomb in your tummy?'

'Pretty much,' Lee said, thinking that sounded impressive.

'Did it hurt?' Kate asked.

Lee thought it best to suggest he could take pain in his stride if he was to be their commander-in-chief. He shrugged. 'Well, you know how it is ... You just have to grin and bear it.'

'So what are the tubes for?' Scott asked.

'To remove all the poison.'

'You got poisoned, too?'

'The explosion caused it.'

'Man, you really have been in the wars.'

'These things happen,' Lee said matter-of-factly. He turned to Andrew. 'What about you?'

'Oh, I broke my leg and I've had to have a pin put in it,' Andrew explained.

'How big is it?' Kate asked.

'The same size as the other one,' Andrew replied.

'Not your leg, dummy. The pin!'

'Oh, I see what you mean.' Andrew moved his fingers about ten centimetres apart. 'About that size.'

His audience was aghast.

'Why do you need it?' Scott asked.

'It's to do with the way my leg was fractured.'

'Will it be there for the rest of your life?'

'I don't know yet.'

'Does that mean the alarm will go off every time you go

through the metal detector at the airport?' Lee asked, causing everyone to laugh, even Andrew himself until he realised that maybe it was true.

Their medical ailments discussed, it was time to move on to what had brought them together.

'Now,' Lee said, 'I presume Kate has made you aware of the problem with the Consul Mutants.'

Scott and Andrew nodded.

'Well, obviously we can't tackle them head on. We're hardly fighting fit and we're probably outnumbered. So what I suggest is that we gather some intelligence first.'

'My sister's quite brainy,' Andrew said. 'What about her?'

Lee tried to hide his frustration. 'No, no. I mean gather intelligence on the Mutants – where they go, what they do, how they operate, that sort of thing. That way we might be able to work out their weaknesses.'

'Good idea,' Scott said.

'But how are we going to do it?' Andrew asked. 'You're stuck in bed for a start.'

'You guys – oh, and you, too, Kate – will need to do the best you can. I realise you're not as mobile as you'd like to be but that can't be helped.'

'It might mean they won't see you as a threat,' Kate pointed out.

'Yeah, good point,' Lee admitted, wishing he'd thought of it himself.

'So what should we do?' Scott asked. 'Just sort of wander around?'

'Follow the Mutants. When they leave the ward go with them. Pretend you're going to the toilet and then look to see where they go. They must have a base and we need to find out where it is.'

'What about you?' Andrew asked. 'What'll you do?'

'I'll obviously help once these tubes are out and I can move about. But meantime I've got a friend who might be able to assist us. I'll try to contact him. If you can obtain the information we need then he might be able to provide us with technical support.'

'What does that mean?' Kate asked.

'Oh, you know ... essential equipment.'

'Such as ...?'

'Well I don't know yet. I won't know what's essential until you've gathered the intelligence.' He knew it wasn't a very good answer, but it was the only one he could think of. The truth was, he didn't yet know what help Will could be but was sure there'd be a role for him at some point.

'Is that it then?' Kate asked, 'because my favourite programme's on in a minute.'

It was typical of a girl to be more interested in a TV programme than in defending the world against evil invaders from another planet. Girls had no sense of priority.

'Well ... yes. I suppose that's all for now. Let's meet back here at fifteen hundred hours tomorrow.' (The twenty-four hour clock was one thing Lee had paid attention to in class.)

They all agreed and went their separate ways before anyone became suspicious about their group. Scott wheeled himself up the ward while Andrew hobbled along behind like a drunk trying to walk in a straight line. Kate was the only one who stayed at Lee's bedside.

'Do you think they'll be any good as spies?' she asked.

'Hmm,' Lee answered.

However, Scott and Andrew turned out to be better spies than Lee had anticipated.

'The Mutants go through these doors into secret rooms,' an excited Scott told the gang of four at Lee's bedside. 'They go in but don't come out again, so they must have secret passages somewhere. Either that or they can make themselves invisible ... '

'It can't be that,' Kate was quick to point out, 'because you'd still see the doors open and close even if you couldn't see them going through them.'

'But what if they can go through walls,' Andrew suggested.

'That would be awkward,' Lee said. 'We'd never be able to follow them if they could do that.'

'I reckon they must have special portals that take them straight to their spaceship,' Scott said.

'How do you know they've got a spaceship?' Kate asked.

'Of course they have,' Scott said. 'Whoever heard of alien invaders without spaceships? How else would they get here in the first place?'

'Through the portals,' Kate replied calmly. 'If they have

portals they could go straight to another world. So maybe they've found a portal in their world that brings them straight to ours.'

Andrew spoke up. 'But wouldn't someone have discovered the one at this end by now?'

Lee took control again. 'For the moment let's accept that they seem to be able to disappear from view and that we don't know how they do it. We can investigate it further.' He turned to Andrew. 'Have you got anything to report?'

'I tried to follow one of them down the corridor outside the ward, but he was too fast for me.'

That came as no surprise. Lee had seen snails on a go-slow moving faster than Andrew on crutches. However, he hid his disappointment. At least Andrew had tried.

'Oh, but I did find out that they've taken over other wards, not just ours,' Andrew said suddenly.

'How did you find that out?' Lee asked.

'I heard two nurses talking about it, and they weren't from our ward. I'd never seen them before.'

'What did they say?' Kate prompted.

'They said the Consul Mutants treated them like skivvies.'

'Skivvies,' Scott mused. 'Are those people from the planet Skiv?'

'I don't know,' Andrew said. 'I hadn't thought about that.'

'Hey, you dummies,' Kate said. 'A skivvy is someone who's forced to do all the work.'

'So you mean they've taken over Skiv and enslaved all its inhabitants?' Scott said.

Kate looked to the ceiling before answering. 'No, but it does mean the nurses think the Mutants are treating them like slaves.'

'That's interesting, though,' Lee interrupted before Scott or Andrew had time to get in a huff with Kate over her attitude. 'Because we thought none of the adults knew about the Mutants, but if the nurses were talking about them then they must know, only they're unable to resist their orders.'

'That's right,' Andrew agreed.

'Their powers must be really strong,' Scott observed.

'Maybe,' Lee responded, 'but we'll still find a way to defeat them.' He liked that sentence; it sounded like the sort of thing a strong leader would say.

'How?' Kate asked.

'Ah ... Well I haven't actually worked that out yet.'

It was Medicine Time again – a time Lee hated.

All the kids went through the same routine each day.

Around two o'clock Doctor Donald and Nurse Chicken would come into the ward, bringing with them a trolley full of tablets, solutions and, worst of all, syringes.

An injection a day keeps the bugs at bay, Nurse Chicken would say, but to Lee's way of thinking it only gave you a sore bum.

All the able-bodied kids gathered in the middle of the ward, excited despite the fact that it was Medicine Time, which only went to show how dull life was for them normally. Some kids would try to show how tough they were by insisting on going first. *Hey, look at me, I'm cool, I can take the pain*, they were obviously trying to say, but Lee just thought they were stupid. Pain was something to be avoided for as long as possible.

For those like Lee who couldn't get out of their beds, going first or last wasn't an issue. You went when Doctor Donald and Nurse Chicken arrived at your bedside, all smiling and jolly and ready to stick a needle in your rear end. How sad was that? They obviously looked forward to inflicting pain on kids.

Of course Lee realised the main reason Nurse Chicken was smiling so broadly (and giggling a lot, too) was that she fancied Doctor Donald. He knew that because Kate had told him the first time they'd met. It was the sort of mushy nonsense girls were interested in, whereas Lee always covered his eyes with a cushion from the sofa whenever people started kissing on TV.

He had to admit, however, that Nurse Chicken was really pretty and good fun and had a happy, smiling face even when Doctor Donald wasn't with her. She'd usually tell a good joke while sticking a needle into Lee's bum, so that he didn't know whether to laugh or cry. (He usually did both and claimed the moistness around his eyes was from tears of laughter.) Lee reckoned that Nurse Chicken was just desperate to get married so she could get a new surname. And let's face it, who could blame her.

'Your first name's Kerry, isn't it?' Lee asked her as he rolled down his pyjama trousers and pointed his bum in her direction.

'It is,' Nurse Chicken said.

'And have you got a middle name?'

'Yes ... '

'What is it then?'

'Francis.'

'Kerry Francis Chicken,' Lee said.

'Yes ... '

'KFC!'

'Yes, that's right, Lee,' she said in a voice that made it clear she'd heard this a million times before. 'Kentucky Fried Chicken. Very funny.'

Dead right it was! His nurse had the same initials as a fast food restaurant! What on earth had her parents been thinking of? Were they naturally cruel or had they been very drunk when they'd named her? Were their names Hilary Hen and Ken Cockerel, or were they just so stupid they didn't even realise what they'd done?

But then it dawned on Lee that it was even worse than that, because Nurse Chicken fancied Doctor Donald. Doctor Mac Donald! They couldn't get married, not with those names!

Lee laughed out loud but felt his injection was a little sorer than usual, which he doubted was a coincidence.

That evening Lee's mum and dad came to visit, bringing Rebecca with them.

'Hi there, Bunnychops,' his mum beamed, reaching down to kiss him.

Now that the curtains round his bed had been pulled back Lee could see the full length of the ward, which was great except when your mum was going all slushy on you. Kate grinned broadly at him from the seat beside her bed.

There was worse to come.

'Do you want to give Lee a kiss?' his mum asked Rebecca and, before Lee had time to object, Rebecca was pecking his cheek.

Rebecca could be a real pain. She would attack anyone Lee tried to bring into the house, hitting and kicking them. She thought it was a great game. Lee didn't. She was young and a girl, so no-one wanted to hit her back. They tried to hide instead – usually in their own homes. Only Will braved the onslaught these days.

Now that Lee's street cred – or ward cred, in this case – had been reduced to an all-time low with a kiss from his little sister, could his dad help salvage it?

'Lee, I've brought you these,' he said, bringing out a hand from behind his back. In it was a large, padded envelope. He tipped it upside down and shook the contents onto Lee's bed. 'Your teacher brought them round. They're cards from your classmates.'

Ward cred salvaged! Fan mail, that was the proper term for all this post. Hundreds of kids out there were finding it hard to live without him.

'Do you want to open them now?' his mum asked.

'Or maybe you'd like to wait until later,' his dad suggested. 'To give yourself something to do once we've gone.'

He supposed that would be the right thing to do. After all, his family had taken time out to visit him.

'So how are things?' his dad asked.

'Yeah, fine.' What else could he say? He hadn't moved from his bed for two days and nothing much had changed. The boy nearest the TV had been allowed home, but that was it, nothing exciting had happened.

'It sounds as if they're hoping to remove your tube early next week,' his mum said. 'That'll be good, won't it. You'll be able to move around a bit more instead of having to stay in bed all the time.'

'Yeah,' Lee said, thinking more about the possibilities mobility would open up than about his answer.

'Will you have to go in a wheelchair?' Rebecca asked him.

'What? No, I'll be able to walk alright,' Lee told her sharply.

'She was only asking,' his mum said and so he was forced to say sorry.

'You might find it tricky at first,' his dad said.

'I've only been in bed for a couple of weeks,' Lee pointed out. Did his dad think he'd forgotten so quickly how to walk?

'Even so. You'd be surprised how quickly you lose the power of your limbs when you don't use them.'

Lee wondered if the same thing applied to brains. If so,

it explained a lot about a couple of his classmates.

'I'll be fine, Dad. Don't worry.'

Rebecca was renowned for being unable to sit still for more than ten seconds, so by now she'd already beaten her own record. But the strain was too much and she wandered away down the ward, Lee's mum setting off after her, leaving Lee alone with his dad.

'So are you bearing up?' his dad asked.

'Yeah. I'm fine,' Lee told him. 'Can Will come in and see me again?'

'Sure.'

'Soon?'

'Like tomorrow?'

'That would be great!'

'Okay, I'll speak to his parents and see what he's up to.'

What Will was up to was trying to find all those things he'd hidden from his parents over the years but which he now wanted to make sure he took with him to his new home. He began telling Lee this the next evening when Lee's dad went to get a paper from the shop downstairs.

'Right, right,' Lee said, desperate to get on. 'Fascinating though that is, I need to update you on everything that's happened *here* – before Dad gets back.'

'Why, what's ...?'

'It's the Consul Mutants. We think they might be able to travel from their planet to ours using portals.'

'Wow! Have you seen one of their portals?'

'No, I haven't been able to move from my bed, have I. But Scott thinks he saw one.' Lee pointed to Scott, who noticed them both and waved.

'What happened to his hair?' Will said under his breath after turning back to Lee. 'Did one of the Mutants cut it for him? Maybe that style's all the rage on planet Zog, but it's the pits here.'

'I know, I know. But beggars can't be choosers. There weren't many other able-bodied men to choose from, most of the others are confined to bed, like me. And anyway, just because he looks like Friar Tuck doesn't make him a bad spy,' Lee pointed out, a bit defensively.

'I only said his hair's dire, that's all,' Will said.

'Aw,' Lee said, predictably.

There was a tense silence between them for a moment, then Will said, 'Why don't I take a look?'

'You can't go and stare at his hair!'

'Don't be daft, I mean have a look around the *hospital*.'

'How can you?' Lee asked. 'You're just a visitor.'

'What's to stop me wandering around?'

'Eh ... all the staff.'

'I'm only a kid, though. If I go somewhere I'm not supposed to I can just say I got lost and no-one will be bothered.'

'Hmm,' Lee said, and for once he said it because thoughts were starting to occur to him. Good thoughts. Useful thoughts. But above all, sneaky thoughts.

However, Will didn't know this. He assumed it meant – as it usually did – that Lee wasn't convinced, and so he pressed on. 'I could check to see if there really are portals and to see how the Mutants operate them. I could even go into one if I can figure out how it works, and then I could see for sure what's on the other side.'

'Yes,' Lee enthused. 'And you could check out their laboratories, too. We think they've been making poison to get people ill so they have to be taken into hospital.'

'Really?'

'Yes. It makes sense. Once they've poisoned them they can drag some of the patients back to their own planet.'

'What for?'

'I don't know. Maybe to use as circus freaks to entertain the other aliens.'

'You reckon?'

'I don't know, which is all the more reason for us to find out.'

'Right.'

'And they have this machine called Fred,' Lee said, really on a roll now, 'that they use to look inside people to make sure the poison is in the right place in their bodies. They used it on me, but I managed to survive.'

'Wow!' Will was impressed.

'Yeah, they disguise it as a fancy stereo, only it's a rubbish disguise because anyone can tell you can't play CDs on it.'

Lee realised he was wasting valuable time. 'If you're going to go then you'd better go now, before Dad gets back. I'll say you've gone to the toilet.'

Will wasted no time at all. He set off down the ward, walking at the sort of pace that would get him into the Olympic speed-walking team if he could keep it up for ten kilometres.

And he was only just in time. Lee's dad appeared through the doors so soon after Will had exited them that Lee thought they must have met.

But they hadn't.

'Where's Will?' Lee's dad asked, scanning the ward as if he had X-ray vision.

'Eh, he was dying for a poo,' Lee said. 'Too many portions

of beans with his baked potato at lunchtime.' Lee hoped the extra detail would make his story more convincing.

'Beans,' his dad said. 'I wondered what the smell was in the car on the way here. Still, at least if it's beans they shouldn't take long to get through his system.'

'Oh, I don't know. Sometimes they can take quite a while ...'

When Will still hadn't shown up ten minutes later, Lee's dad said, 'Do you think he's alright? Maybe I should go and check. If he's been sitting on the loo all this time he's probably lost the use of his legs.'

'He'll be fine, Dad. His insides are probably just not, you know ... not moving as quickly as normal.' This wasn't a conversation Lee wanted to get into with his dad.

'Hmm. Poor kid. Probably thinks he's trying to pass a brick,' Lee's dad informed him. 'Not enough fibre in his diet, that's what it is. Too much white bread, not enough brown.'

Lee knew for a fact that Will's family only *ever* ate brown bread because Will's mum was a bit of a nut when it came to health foods. That was why Will always had baked potatoes at lunchtime, because they were much better for you than ... well, hot dogs, for instance. Whenever Lee ate at Will's house he would be told exactly how much fat there was in what he was eating. Even though it was usually hardly any, Lee had to admit the food tasted good. Will was always saying his mum was on a diet, and that that was why she knew about all that health stuff, however Lee thought it was a strange diet, because he sometimes saw Will's mum reaching into a kitchen drawer to sneak a bit of chocolate when she thought no-one was looking.

For the next five minutes Lee was forced to endure an update from his dad on all the excitement he'd missed out on at home: the mowing of the lawn, the planting of some lovely nasturtiums (which were plants that had flowers you could eat, according to his dad, though Lee said he really couldn't see himself choosing them over a chocky biscuit when it came to snack time); the washing of the car after a flock of birds used it for target practice and covered it in droppings; how Rebecca had painted a really lovely picture for the 'Paint a Really Lovely Picture' contest at school ...

In other words, he hadn't missed much.

'Now I really had better go and find Will,' Lee's dad said, looking worried. 'Are you sure he knows where the toilets are?'

'If he doesn't he'll probably be searching for a new pair of trousers by now.'

Lee's dad rose and walked quickly out of the ward.

Ten seconds later he was back again. And Will was with him.

'Found him,' Lee's dad said as they approached the bed. (Sometimes he said the most obvious things.) 'You hadn't flushed yourself down the toilet after all, had you, Will. You were just waving a friend off to the sea.'

'What ...?' Lee began to ask but then began laughing, as did Will.

'Apparently it was an emotional farewell,' Lee's dad added. 'The "friend" really didn't want to leave.' He looked at Will. 'How many flushes did you say it took to send him off?'

'Eh ...' Will said, and Lee could easily tell he was just making it up. 'Six.'

'Six!' Lee's dad said. 'An aircraft carrier could float in that amount of water.'

No-one said anything for a few seconds, Will because he was too embarrassed and Lee because he couldn't believe what his dad was saying.

'I need to go myself now after talking about it,' Lee's dad declared, and headed off again, leaving Lee and Will alone, which was extremely convenient because they wanted to talk.

'Were you really in the toilet all that time?' Lee asked as soon as his dad was out of hearing distance.

'No, of course not,' Will told him. 'I went in there on the way back.'

'Good plan.'

'It wasn't a *plan*. I was desperate!'

'You mean you couldn't find the portal anywhere else and thought it must be in the toilet?'

'No, no, I was desperate for a number two. It must have been that extra portion of beans I had with my baked potato at lunchtime.'

Aha!

'And the six flushes ...?'

'Don't be stupid! That was just to explain how long I'd taken.'

Lee remembered they didn't have long before his dad would return. 'So what did you find out, then?' he asked.

'Loads,' Will replied. 'Loads and loads.' And so he told him exactly what that loads was, and it was loads more than the loads Lee had been expecting.

'And I saw that creepy guy again.'

'Which one?'

'The tall one. The one that passed us the other day.'

'Doctor Enleader?'

'Yes. He came up the corridor behind me. It was as if he was following me.'

'Hmm. Maybe they're suspicious about us. We'll need to be careful.'

Lee's dad returned. 'We'll need to get going,' he said.

'I haven't had my dinner yet. Okay?'

'Oh. Right,' Lee said. 'I suppose so.' It would have been good if Will could have stayed for longer, but given the loads of stuff Will had told Lee about, Lee was just as happy to have time to mull it all over.

Lee's dad picked up his paper and patted Lee on the shoulder. 'Mum'll be in tomorrow,' he said, and with that they started walking away from Lee's bed, Will in front.

But then Lee's dad stopped, leaving Will to walk on. 'By the way, Lee,' he said over his shoulder. 'How did you know what Will had for lunch if you weren't even there?'

Chapter
Seven

Lee awoke next morning so famished he could have eaten a scabby-headed baby. So it was as well that they kept them in a separate ward. Instead he ate two bacon rolls smothered in an entire bottle of tomato sauce.

The only thing about bacon rolls is that they're salty, so you have to drink lots of water to quench your thirst.

The only problem about drinking lots of water to quench your thirst is that it makes you want the toilet all the time.

And the only thing about wanting the toilet all the time when you're stuck in bed is that you can't go.

Well that's not strictly true. Obviously you have to *do* the toilet – they can hardly expect you to hold it in for weeks on end. Can you imagine what your legs would be like by the time you got out? They wouldn't so much be crossed as tied in the sort of really really really strong knot you learn in the Cubs. And they'd need to be! Unless, that is, they gave you a huge pair of waterproof pants that went all the way down to the bottom of your legs, with elastic around the ankles...so that your pee couldn't get out. Then it would be fine, you could just lie in bed and pee away! And it would have another benefit, too: it would keep your legs warm! But can you imagine the flooding when you finally took them off?

So, if you're a boy, hospitals have another solution.

You pee into a milk bottle!

Well, it's not actually a milk bottle, of course, because it wouldn't be very hygienic if you went to pour milk on your cereal and ...

No, no, let's not go there. You get the message.

So they're not real milk bottles, but they do look a bit like them, and you have to hold them under your covers while you have a pee AND you have to try to make sure you aim straight. Because, if you miss the bottle, they send the most grumpy, most moody nurses in the whole hospital to change your manky, stinking, soaking sheets.

Which is why Lee was lying on a stretcher trolley next to his bed with the hospital's two most grumpy, most moody and, it must be said, most downright ugly nurses changing his manky, stinking bedclothes. (And these nurses weren't averagely ugly, they were *really* ugly, with faces like cows – and not the end that eats the grass!)

'Och, these are absolutely distgusting,' one nurse said in the loudest voice Lee had ever heard. 'I think I'm going to barf.'

'I'm not allowed to have one,' Lee said.

'What?' she yelled.

'I'm not allowed a bath – in case I get my dressing wet ... '
He pointed to his wound.

'Bath? Who said anything about a bath?' she said.

'Well, didn't you ... '

And then it dawned on Lee that she really did mean barf.

The other nurse seemed to think she'd better have a good moan too - in case her colleague got ahead in the Moaning Premier League. 'These sheets of yours are absolutely ringing. What did you do? Go for a swim and accidentally drink the pool?'

'Sorry,' Lee said. 'I...eh...got caught out.'

Fortunately the nurses had drawn the curtains around his bed. Lee just hoped Kate wasn't lying on her bed next door listening to what was being said.

However there was no mention of the need to change bedclothes as the third Council of War got under way later that day, so Lee relaxed and focused instead on the vital intelligence Will had brought back the previous evening.

The others were eager to hear it. Lee had hinted he had something important to tell them but hadn't said what it was, so they were all intrigued.

'Did he find out something new?' Andrew asked.

'He certainly did.'

'Well don't keep us in suspenders,' Scott said. 'Tell us what it is.'

'Okay. Well, Will was walking down one of the corridors when he saw a room full of ... ' Even Lee was excited by the news.

'Of what?' the others asked in unison.

'Of arms and legs.'

The others stared blankly until finally Kate said, 'You mean ... just arms and legs, nothing else?'

'The Mutants must be small creatures that don't normally walk or have hands!' Andrew exclaimed.

'Exactly!'

'Maybe their planet isn't like ours,' Andrew went on. 'Maybe it's all under the sea and they just swim around all the time, but when they come to ours they need to use the arms and legs to be able to get around.'

'And they have to look like us,' Scott chipped in, 'because otherwise they'd scare us and we'd attack them or something.'

Kate picked up the thread. 'And maybe they don't need arms and legs where they live because they can get things to do whatever they want just by thinking about them doing it.'

'Mind control!' Andrew declared. 'The same way they can get all the doctors and nurses to do what they want when they're in our world.'

They all understood the importance of Will's discovery, so now Lee could reveal his plan.

It was, of course, a cunning plan. So cunning that even cunning Consul Mutants wouldn't be cunning enough to guess it.

That evening Lee decided to open his fan mail. He'd forgotten about it in all the excitement of Will's discovery and the Council of War meeting afterwards.

He tipped up the big padded envelope and a stack of smaller envelopes scattered themselves over his bed.

His classmates were obviously missing him dreadfully. And to think he'd always considered himself invisible around school. How wrong he'd been. It seemed the truth was that other pupils were in awe of him. They didn't speak to him because they thought they might make themselves look stupid given his superior intellect and charm. If only he'd realised sooner.

He opened the first envelope. In it was a card of the sort

that could only be made in class. Cut out shapes of ... well, something. It was difficult to tell what they were supposed to be. Lee turned the card upside down in case that made it any clearer. It didn't. So he prised apart the glue-stuck sides.

Dear Lea,
Hop your having a nice tim in hopsital.
Craig

Oh, yeah, Craig, it's great! You should try it yourself! Get a terrible illness just so you can come and see what it's like! It's a holiday, and you don't even have to pay for it!

PS Keep practising your spelling.

He ought to introduce Craig to Scott with two 't's. He'd soon sharpen him up.

Lee moved on to the next envelope, hoping for better things.

Dear Le,
Missing you a lot NOT!
Jamie

Oh, ha ha, very funny. Well at least Jamie's drawing on

the front was recognisable. It was a dragon. Jamie always drew dragons. He drew them on all his jotters even though The Ogre shouted at him because of it.

Dear Leee,
I was in hospital once, too. I hated it.
Love Emily

Dear Lee,
I hope you don't die.
Love from Holly

For what it was worth, Lee felt the same way.

Dear Lee,
School just isn't the same without you.
Its much better!
From Ryan

Wow, two in a row who'd spelt his name correctly!
Lee had never liked Ryan much anyway.

He decided not to open any more. He would quit while he was ahead. And maybe he would stay in hospital for a good while longer, because it didn't sound like anyone was too keen to have him back.

Lee's mum popped in on her way home from working late in the office.

'Hi, Shmoochkins. How are you today?'

'Fine,' Lee said, knowing that was what his mum wanted to hear. ('Terrible. None of my classmates like me and I'm probably going to die,' wouldn't, he didn't think, give her the same measure of reassurance.)

His mum suddenly seemed to be looking for something around his bed.

'What? What is it?' Lee asked.

'Oh, I thought you might have put up some of your nice cards.'

'Ah ... well there were so many that I couldn't fit them all in.'

Lee did have a lot of nice cards. Some of the pictures were lovely and artistic and almost good enough to enter in the sort of Make a Lovely and Artistic Card Competition Lee's little sister would have loved. It was just the messages inside them that Lee wasn't so keen on.

'Oh, that's a shame. What have you done with them?'

'I, eh ... shared them around.'

His mum was puzzled. 'You shared them around?'

'Yeah, some of the other kids haven't received any cards at all, so I gave them some of mine.'

His mum still looked puzzled. Even more so than before.

'But Cuddlekins, don't they think it's a bit strange receiving Get Well Soon cards with *your* name on them?'

Lee's alarm bells were ringing. He was in the midst of one of those lies that starts small and simple but becomes more and more complicated until it takes over your life, and he couldn't see a way out.

But then he had a flash of inspiration.

'Most of the other kids can't read,' he told his mum. 'So they think the cards are actually for them.'

'Oh,' his mum said. '*None* of them can read? Really?'

'Yeah, so don't you think it was a really good idea,' he enthused, trying to convince her.

'Well, yes, I suppose it was very ... well, thoughtful of you.'

Lee shrugged as if that was just the sort of kid he was – putting others before himself, giving away his possessions without a thought for his own needs, concerned only to ensure the poor had food to eat and the ill had proper medical care and that the truth never got in the way of a good story.

The next day, Doctor Donald brought unwelcome news.

No, it wasn't that another batch of cards had been delivered. It was much worse than that.

'Lee,' Doctor Donald said as he stood at the side of the bed, 'we've found another area of infection.'

Infection was a bad thing. Infection meant more medicine and more injections.

'But how?' Lee asked, worried. 'I thought you blasted it all.'

'Well this sort of thing isn't easy to diagnose, even with all the equipment we've got – like the ultrasound.'

'Fred, you mean.'

'Eh, yeah ... Fred. That's right. You see, Lee, sometimes when your appendix bursts it sends poison to different parts of your body. And if you've been lying down – like you have been – it can occasionally get in behind your lungs. It doesn't happen very often, but it's happened in your case. It's what's been giving you that chesty cough.'

Lungs, thought Lee. Weren't they essential for breathing? And wasn't breathing essential for staying alive?

'Am I going to die?' he asked, trying to work out how much pocket money he'd saved and whether it would be enough to pay for his funeral.

Doctor Donald gave a chuckle. 'No, I don't think you need to worry about that. We'll need to adjust your tube and give you some slightly different medicine, but I'm sure you'll be fine. It just means you'll be with us for a little longer than we first planned.'

Judging from the cards he'd received during the first week of his stay, no-one in his class would notice if he didn't return for quite a while. Or if they did it would be because they were glad to be rid of him, so maybe being in hospital wasn't such a bad thing ... except that he'd miss Will, of course, and ...

What was he thinking of! He suddenly realised he was being taken in. This was all part of the Consul Mutants' plan to sneak him off through the portal to their planet. He'd be a perfect candidate. Someone no-one would really miss. Someone they could make disappear without it even making the news headlines.

'Okay?' Doctor Donald asked, concerned, when Lee hadn't spoken for about twenty seconds.

'Eh, yeah,' Lee said. He'd decided he ought to make them think he hadn't figured out their plan. 'Fine.'

Doctor Donald nodded and continued on his rounds.

But of course everything wasn't 'fine'. Everything was

terrible. He was about to be taken to another planet and, once there, made to work as a slave. Or maybe they would cut off his arms and legs and give them to Mutants who wanted to go to Earth but couldn't because all the arms and legs in the hospital were already booked up.

Lee had to think of a plan. And quickly!

And he did think of a plan. Extremely quickly. In under a minute, in fact, which was pretty good for the sort of plan he'd come up with.

The logic behind his plan was that the Mutants would only take kids no-one would notice were missing. Knowing this, all Lee had to do was transform himself into someone *everyone* would notice was missing so he wouldn't go missing in the first place.

Brilliant!

Except for one small point.

Which was that for his entire life Lee had been trying to become more noticeable to other kids, and he *still* hadn't succeeded.

However, Lee had often heard his dad say, 'where there's a will there's a way.' And when he thought about this it all became so obvious. Where there was a *Will* there was a way. Of course! Will was the key to it all. Will would help make Lee's name known throughout the hospital and beyond, and then Lee would be able to escape the evil tyranny of the Mutants.

So, Lee's plan could be summarised as: ask Will what to do.

Which, like a few of Lee's other plans, actually wasn't much of a plan at all.

But it became a better plan once Will heard that his help was required.

'I know just what to do,' Will told him.

'What?' Lee asked, excited.

'I'll need to check everything first, but I think it might just work.'

'What might, Will? What are you? ... Oh, hi Mum.'

Bad timing. It was too late for Will to tell him.

The next day was really boring. It dragged on and on, like the sort of walks your parents take you on, making you stop to look at glorious flowers and wonderful views and fantastic houses. Indeed it was so boring that by five-thirty in the afternoon getting an injection in his bum had been the highlight of Lee's day.

He couldn't even talk to the others, because Kate, Andrew and Scott all had visitors. So Lee reached over and turned on the radio beside his bed to save himself from the dullness of listening to other people's conversations.

'Welcome to Hospital FM, the radio station for your hospital,' said an annoyingly happy voice. *'For the next few hours we'll be playing some of your all-time favourite music, as well as your requests. And here's one of them. This is for Melista Thingstobuy – unusual name you've got there, Melista – and it's that all-time classic, Jailhouse Rock, by the King himself.'*

That was impressive, thought Lee. Getting royalty to sing especially for a Hospital FM listener. Melista was obviously either on her last legs or related to the Royal Family.

The song crackled out and Lee found himself tapping his

foot in time to the beat.

'The King there, having a great time at a party at the county jail.' Lee was even more impressed. The King was mixing with prison inmates, singing them songs to help their years behind bars pass more quickly ... What a guy!

'Later today, in a special feature, we'll be meeting up with a real boy wonder who's currently with us in the hospital, and who holds the World Rice-Krispie-eating record at an amazing seven bowls in one breakfast sitting. That's certainly one to look forward to, folks.'

Lee was stunned into silence, even though he hadn't been speaking. He was going to be on the radio!

But how? And why? (And who, what, where and when, for that matter.)

'Will!' Lee whispered to himself, suddenly realising what was happening. This was what Will was going to tell him about the day before. This was his plan! And it was a plan only a genius like Will could have come up with. Once Lee had been interviewed on Hospital FM no-one would be able to touch him, not even the Consul Mutants. He'd be famous – sufficiently so that if he were to disappear it would raise suspicions. *Mutants Kidnap Cereal-Eating Champion* the newspaper headlines would cry out on their front pages, and the cover of the Mutants would be blown.

The United Nations would muster the armies of the world to track down every Consul Mutant that had already made it to Earth and, after confiscating their arms and legs, would banish the Mutants back to their own world.

Lee was so absorbed in thinking about Will's plan that he didn't notice the DJ approaching his bed. It was only when he was right next to him that Lee realised who he must be.

Lee knew DJs were cool because he listened to them on the radio at home and in the car (when he could persuade his parents not to listen to someone droning on about politics or gardening). DJs had voices that made everything sound really special, and they knew everything there was to know about music, including how to make that scratching sound with records. They also dressed in trendy clothes, had up-to-the-minute haircuts, drove flash cars and got to meet loads of famous people.

Yes, DJs were brilliant. And Lee was about to be interviewed by one!

Only this one didn't quite fit with Lee's impression of what a DJ ought to be like. For a start, he was about the same age as Lee's dad. Secondly, he had a belly that made him look as if he'd stuffed all of his bedclothes – including the duvet – up his T-shirt and then thrown in a bag of potatoes for good measure. Thirdly, he was wearing glasses so big and thick that Lee's parents could have double-glazed most of their house with them. Had it not been for the headphones covering his ears, Lee wouldn't have recognised him as a DJ at all.

In his hand the DJ was carrying what looked like a dead rabbit on a stick. It was big and grey and hairy. Lee wondered if perhaps it was fluff that had gathered in the man's belly button. Maybe having an enormous stomach meant his belly button went so deep that he needed to use a stick to get the fluff out.

'Yo, Lee,' the man said, sounding more like a teacher trying to be hip than like a DJ. Then he held out the belly button candyfloss to Lee.

For a few seconds Lee wasn't sure what was expected. Was he meant to take a bite?

Then he realised it was a microphone. 'Oh, right. Eh, yo DJ,' Lee said in a rush.

'Okay, how was that?'

'Fine, thanks,' Lee said.

'I'm talking to my engineer,' the DJ said.

'Pardon?' Lee was confused but remembered his manners. (His parents would have been proud.)

'How's the level?' the DJ asked.

'Well, I'd rather sit,' Lee said, propping himself up against his pillows. However, the DJ didn't seem to be listening. It was as if he was hearing voices in his head.

Meanwhile, Lee's visitor had not gone unnoticed by the other kids on the ward. There was a lot of pointing in the direction of Lee's bed, and then small groups of children began creeping closer, fascinated.

Suddenly the DJ burst into life. Lee heard him in stereo – in person and through the radio at his bedside. The voice was completely different now. It had far more energy and finally Lee could almost believe the man before him was a proper DJ.

'Well, here I am on Ward Nine at the bedside of a kid called Lee, who I'm reliably informed holds the hospital's cereal-eating record. Lee, tell all the Hospital FM listeners just how many bowls of cereal you ate in one breakfast sitting!'

The DJ nodded at Lee to speak, but Lee was too busy watching the others kids as their shyness disappeared and they gathered around. Obviously only those who could leave their beds could actually surround Lee's. The remainder were left to gaze on from afar, probably risking death or electrocution (or both) by stretching their tubes and cables to get as close as possible. It was like the time he'd been carried to the ambulance and all the local kids had flocked to see what was happening.

'Lee?' the DJ prompted impatiently. 'Are you going to tell us how many bowls you ate? Or have you had a tongue bypass?'

'What? Oh, eh, right. Eh, seven,' Lee eventually said.

The DJ turned to the other kids. 'Yes, folks, seven bowls!' He turned back to Lee. 'And let the listeners into your secret, Lee. What kind of cereal did you eat to break the record?'

'Rice Krispies.'

'And had you been training for months before making this record attempt?'

'No.'

'Weeks, then?'

'No.'

The DJ seemed to have lost his words for a second, but then found them again. 'Now, as you say, you ate Rice Krispies to break the record. Did you choose them in particular for your record attempt because they are made almost entirely from air, making them less filling than some other cereals?'

'No.'

'No? Well was it because they go all mushy in milk, making

it easier to eat lots of them?'

'No.'

The DJ seemed to be getting annoyed. 'I'll tell you what, Lee, to save me spending the rest of the programme going through all the possible alternatives, why don't you just tell all the Hospital FM listeners your reason for using Rice Krispies in your record attempt.'

The belly button candyfloss was offered up to Lee again. 'Because I like them,' Lee said.

'Oh yes indeed. There you have it, folks. Lee used Rice Krispies because he likes them.'

There were a few sniggers from around the bed at the DJ's sarcastic tone.

'Well Lee, it's been incredible speaking to you. I'm sure the listeners have learned loads from what you've told us.' The DJ started to move away, speaking as he went. 'That's Lee there, folks. Lee the talkative champion cereal eater. Obviously his mouth is still too worn out from chomping those Krispies for him to speak to us in more than two words at a time, so let's get on with another record ... '

With a jolt Lee realised what was happening. The interview was over. The DJ was heading back to his studio. The other kids were walking or limping or hobbling or wheeling themselves back to their beds. The excitement was over, and he'd blown it!

He'd blown it because he'd only spoken sixteen words in total. (He'd been counting.) Sixteen words, of which a quarter had been 'no' and a further eighth had been 'eh', which wasn't even a real word. And 'what' and 'right' had been hesitations, so they didn't count either.

Which left seven words. That was all he'd said that might have meant anything to anyone who was listening. Seven stingy, measly, miserable, pitiful, puny, paltry and pathetic words. (And they hadn't even been seven good words like the adjectives in the previous sentence.)

What was he going to tell Will? He'd given Lee the best chance he would ever get to escape the Mutants and what had Lee done? He'd made a complete and utter mess of it. He'd stood in front of the open goal and kicked the ball past the post. He'd spun his car off the track just as he'd approached the finishing line. He'd dropped the baton when his team were about to win the relay race. He was a plonker, a wally, an idiot, a halfwit and some slightly less flattering names that the kids at school occasionally called him.

Lee could have kicked himself. In fact he did. And it hurt. So he decided not to do it again. A verbal telling off would be sufficient next time.

Next time? What was he thinking of? There wouldn't be a next time. He was a goner. He'd soon be on his way through that portal, never to be seen on Earth ever again. That was it, his one chance had passed. For Lee, this was:

THE END

Of course it wasn't *really* the end. It just felt for a moment as if nothing lay ahead of him other than a blank page.

And anyway, would a superhero like Lee simply give up and allow himself to be carted off to Skiv to become a slave for the rest of his natural life? Of course not.

In any case, Lee would be much better at *using* a slave than being one, whether on Skiv or anywhere else. His mum often used to ask, 'What did your last slave die of?' whenever Lee asked her to do something for him – to which Lee would always answer, 'Working too hard.'

But if fame from being on Hospital FM wasn't going to save Lee he would have to come up with another idea.

However, it was difficult to think about important things – things like saving your life – when someone was fiddling with the tubes sticking out the side of your tummy.

'Hmm,' Nurse Chicken said. 'I don't like the look of this.'

'What?' Lee asked.

'I think your tube might be blocked.' She fiddled about some more. 'No, it definitely looks blocked to me. I'd better get Doctor Donald to take a look.' She stood up. 'Don't go anywhere.'

What a shame, Lee thought. He'd just been about to set out on a fortnight's holiday to Florida.

After a couple of minutes Nurse Chicken was back with Doctor Donald, so her smile was wrapped most of the way around her head.

Lee was still sitting up in bed.

'Now then, Lee,' Doctor Donald said. 'I need to check this tube of yours, so if you can look up at the ceiling for a moment ... '

Lee looked up. It wasn't a very interesting ceiling, but then he already knew that – he'd spent most of the last couple of weeks staring at it.

Doctor Donald twiddled about and then ...

'Yugghh!'

Lee immediately lowered his head. And what he saw was not very pleasant. Not very pleasant at all. In fact Doctor Donald's description was perfect. Yugghh!

Doctor Donald was in the best position to make the description. As he'd tried to unblock Lee's tube the gunk inside had sprayed out onto his hands, arms, chest and, worst of all, his face, where it was now running very slowly down to the end of his chin. Any moment soon it would drip.

'Oh dear,' Nurse Chicken said, offering Doctor Donald a tissue and scrunching up her face in repulsion.

Was this to be the end of their big romance? Would Nurse Chicken become a good deal less excited about kissing Doctor Donald's lips now she'd seen gooey gunk sliding down his face just a couple of centimetres below them?

'Oh, man,' Doctor Donald said, standing with his arms outstretched as if he'd been standing next to a large, deep puddle when a lorry had passed.

Nurse Chicken slotted Lee's tube back into his tummy while Doctor Donald left to clean himself up.

'Poor Doctor Donald,' Nurse Chicken said.

Never mind Doctor Donald! Lee thought. What about me? I'm the one who's got that gunk inside me!

It seemed to Lee that everyone was determined to break his concentration just when he needed it to work out a new plan. No sooner had Nurse Chicken left than a cleaning lady appeared with a mop, swishing it around under his bed and chatting away about nothing in particular. 'What did you have for your breakfast?' she asked, but then before Lee had time to answer she said, 'I had a nice cup of tea and a slice of toast. You can't beat a cup of tea and a slice of toast first thing in the morning, can you?' Again Lee wasn't given time to answer. 'Just the one slice, mind,' she continued, 'because I'm watching my weight these days.'

Lee stared at her. If she was watching her weight then she was surely seeing it increase, because she was almost bursting out of the clothes she was wearing.

And when the cleaner moved on to annoy another patient, Isa came round with afternoon juice and biscuits.

'What's your surname?' Lee asked her.

'Why do you ask?'

'Just wondering,' Lee said.

'Hmm. Well it's Dolittle.'

'Dolittle,' Lee repeated. 'As in ... '

'That's right, as in Doctor Dolittle,' Isa said. 'I come from a lazy family.'

With that she walked away and Lee was finally left alone to consider his options.

'Lee, I've got better news for you this time,' Doctor Donald said, standing at the far end of the bed, out of range of Lee's gunk gun (as he now thought of his tube). We've managed to remove all that fluid behind your lung.' (Lee was sure he could see Doctor Donald cringe at the very thought of that fluid.) 'So in a day or so we should have all these tubes and whatnot removed and you'll be able to move about a bit more.'

'Really?' Lee said, thinking the timing was too good to be true.

'Yep. Your legs will take a while to recover, but at least you'll be mobile again.'

'Brilliant!'

'I thought you'd be pleased. There's nothing worse than being confined to bed, is there.'

There wasn't, so Lee shook his head. Everything was falling into place and now the new plan he'd come up with might just have a chance of working.

'How long will I have to wait?' he asked.

'Let's see. It's Tuesday today and I've scheduled you in for ... ' Doctor Donald checked his notes. ' ... Thursday.'

'Two days.'

'That's right.'

Lee decided he could wait that long.

Nonetheless, those two days dragged. Lee wished away every second of every minute of every hour until he was taken into the operating theatre again and his tubes were removed.

He awoke later the same day feeling groggy, but he soon improved, helped by a light lunch.

'Can I get up now?' Lee asked Nurse Chicken when he saw her.

'Hmm. I'd give your system a chance to recover from the operation first,' she said. 'Maybe tomorrow, yeah?'

Lee resisted the strong temptation to slip out of bed despite Nurse Chicken's advice and tried to concentrate on the bundle of Maths homework he'd been sent by The Ogre. How kind of her to think up such an exciting way to fill his day. She must have known he was addicted to addition, desperate for decimals, glum without graphs, longing for long division, sombre without subtraction and forlorn without fractions.

NOT!

However, he decided that since he had to stay in bed he might as well get his work out of the way. He certainly didn't want to be loaded down with it later, because he had plans. Big plans. Important plans. Planned plans.

'We need to mount a reconnaissance mission,' he told Kate,

Andrew and Scott in the middle of the next morning.

'A what?' Andrew asked.

'We need to locate that secret room Will found,' Lee explained.

'Why?' Kate asked.

'Because that's the key to everything.'

'How is it?'

'Because if we can get into it we can disrupt their whole strategy.'

Kate considered this for a second. 'I still don't ... '

But Lee was already speaking again and didn't stop for Kate. 'Obviously we can't all go because that would be too obvious – they'd know we were up to something. So I'll go,' he said.

'But you can't even walk,' Andrew said. 'How can you go on a reconnaissance mission if you can't walk?'

'Ah, but that's where you're wrong,' Lee replied rather smugly. 'I *can* walk. Doctor Donald said I can get out of bed now if I want.'

'Go on then,' Scott said. 'Let's see you.'

'Okay, I will,' Lee told him, and lifted back the cover on his bed.

'Are you going on the mission right now?' Andrew asked.

'I might as well.'

Lee swung his legs over the side of the bed.

'If I'm not back in twenty minutes send out a search party,' he said. 'But don't tell them why I've gone. I'll make up something if I have to.'

He placed one foot on the ground then planted the other beside it, making sure the side of the bed still bore his weight.

'Right, I'll report back what I find. See you later.'

With those words he set off.

Well, his upper body set off. His legs stayed exactly where he'd put them, on the spot next to the bed.

Lee fell straight to the ground.

Kate, Andrew and Scott laughed their heads off. (Fortunately there were plenty of surgeons on hand to sew them back on.)

'What's so funny?' Lee asked, but that only made the others laugh even more.

He tried pushing himself up with his arms, but his legs just weren't interested in supporting him, so he had to crawl back to the edge of the bed.

'I guess you won't be going on the reconnaissance mission then,' Andrew said when he was finally able to control his sniggering and lend Lee a helping hand to get back onto his bed.

Nurse Chicken arrived on the scene.

'Now then, Lee. What did Doctor Donald warn you?'

'That I wouldn't be able to walk straight away,' Lee mumbled as if The Ogre was telling him off.

'And did you believe him?'

'No.'

'And so what happened when you tried to walk anyway?'

'I fell over.'

Kate, Scott and Andrew burst out laughing again, unable to contain themselves. Even Nurse Chicken couldn't stop herself cackling like a witch, so it wasn't until she was able to wipe away her tears of laughter that she could say, 'So would you like a wheelchair to begin with?'

Another mumble. Lee's ward cred was at an all-time low. 'Yes, please.'

'Okay, I'll get the porters to bring you one.'

Off she strode. Lee could tell she was still giggling because she had her hand up to her mouth and kept leaning forward every few steps.

'That was so funny,' Kate said, finally recovering. 'The back of my head's sore from all that laughing.'

'Mine, too,' Andrew agreed.

'And mine,' Scott chipped in, not to be outdone.

'Yes, well my knees are sore,' Lee told them grumpily. 'And

not from laughter; from landing on them when I fell.'

There were more sniggers until Lee gave them all a hard stare. 'It's not funny, you know.'

The others disagreed and exploded into laughter again.

Lee's wheelchair arrived shortly before lunch. In the meantime he'd tried to build up the strength in his legs by moving them about in the bed and then by dangling them over the side and gradually lowering his weight onto them. He found he could manage a few steps at a time so long as he held on to the bed's metal frame, but it was hard going. He was horrified that three weeks without using his legs had left them in such poor condition, unable even to hold his body weight. He wondered if he'd ever be able to walk properly again.

Even when his wheelchair arrived he discovered that mobility was still difficult to achieve. There was quite a knack to pushing the wheels without jamming your fingers in the spokes and ripping them off. Lee was suddenly very impressed by any wheelchair athlete who could complete all twenty-six miles and three hundred and eighty-five yards of a marathon. Lee could just about manage to propel himself to the end of his bed.

So he had to come up with another solution to his mobility problem. And that solution was to get someone else to push him around. Scott was already in a wheelchair of his own and Andrew could hardly push and hop at the same time, so the someone had to be Kate. Lee wished he didn't have to ask for her help, but he had no other option.

'So we'll need to go on the reconnaissance mission together?' she said.

'Eh, well, yes, I suppose so.'

Kate looked pleased. 'We might as well go now, then,' she said.

Lee had planned on having lunch first but didn't want to sound like a wimp, so he agreed with her.

'Do you know where you're going?' Andrew asked.

'Sort of,' Lee said. 'Down the corridor and then ... well, we'll have a look around.'

'So you don't really know,' Kate said.

'No. But if Will was able to find the room then I'm sure we can.'

Kate shrugged and off they went. Andrew couldn't hop quickly enough to keep up, but Scott rolled alongside in his wheelchair until Lee warned him off. 'You'll draw attention to us,' he whispered. 'Doctor Enleader's already suspicious. We don't want him working out what we're trying to do.'

'What *are* we trying to do?' Kate asked.

'We're trying to work out what we need to do next,' Lee said. It didn't seem a very good explanation but at least it was truthful.

Lee stretched out his arms to push aside the double doors at the end of the ward. It was the first time he'd been through them in a vertical position – every other time he'd been lying on a stretcher, either going to the operating theatre or to see Fred, the Mutants' ultrasound machine – and it looked very different when you weren't staring at the ceiling.

'Where does this corridor lead?' Lee asked Kate.

'That depends,' she said. 'If you go straight on you'll eventually get to the main entrance where all the visitors come in, but if you turn left where those arrows are ... ' She slowed the wheelchair and pointed down the corridor. Lee could see the arrows but the words alongside them on the wall were too small to read from that distance. 'Actually, I'm not very sure,' Kate said. 'I don't think I've ever been up there.'

'Maybe it's where Will went, then.'

'It could be.'

They pushed on and were soon close enough to be able to read the signs.

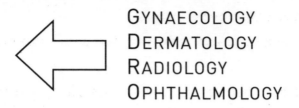

GYNAECOLOGY
DERMATOLOGY
RADIOLOGY
OPHTHALMOLOGY

'What does all that mean?' Lee asked Kate. 'It's all a load of ologies to me. I mean, Dermatology. Why should people called Dermat get a department all to themselves?'

'Isn't ophthalmology something to do with looking at birds?' Kate suggested.

'What? How could that make you better? Although,' Lee said, pointing at the sign, 'I can't see how listening to the radio would help either.'

'So, do you want to go down there?' Kate asked as a pair of nurses passed them.

'Yes,' Lee said, deciding it was time to be decisive.

Kate pushed the handles on the back of the chair until she'd turned it to face up the new corridor. There were more signs further up, and it looked as if there might be smaller corridors running off it.

'A map would be handy,' Lee said, eyeing up all the doors to the left and right. 'This place is like a rabbit's warren.'

As they passed one of the doors a man in a white coat

came out carrying a small box. He seemed surprised to see Lee and Kate in front of him.

'Hello,' he said, blocking their way. 'Are you in the right place?'

Kate responded before the cogs in Lee's head were able to crank an answer out through his mouth. 'We've to get some exercise,' she said. 'The doctor said it would help my leg heal more quickly.'

'Oh, I see. So you're not lost?'

'Lost? No, no. We've been this way lots of times before. It's not as busy, so there's less danger of us bumping into people.'

'Yeah,' Lee said, finally catching up. 'You know what these women drivers are like.'

The man in the white coat laughed. 'Only too well!'

But Kate didn't seem to find it so funny. She leaned over in front of Lee and said, 'Do you want to push yourself back?'

'It was just a joke,' Lee said.

'Hmm,' Kate said. 'Jokes are meant to be funny.'

The man in the white coat rocked back on one foot. 'Right, well, I'll leave you two to argue it out, shall I? I've got to be going.' He set off down the corridor, heading in the direction Lee and Kate had just come from.

'That was close,' Lee said once he was out of earshot. He tried to push himself up in his chair, but he couldn't get high enough to see through the glass panel in the door the man had exited. 'What's through there?' he had to ask Kate.

She stood on her tiptoes because she wasn't very tall. Even then she had to jump a few centimetres.

'I think it's a laboratory of some sort,' she said once she'd jumped a couple of times. 'There are lots of microscopes around the side and racks of test tubes on a table.'

'They probably use it to inject special micro bugs into human brains so people will do whatever the Mutants tell them!'

'You think? This must be the right part of the hospital, then.'

Lee was convinced of it. 'Come on, let's see if we can find the room Will talked about.'

Kate pushed him further along the corridor until they came to a junction. Two signs indicated their choices.

RADIOLOGY
GYNAECOLOGY

OPHTHALMOLOGY
DERMATOLOGY

'Which way?' Kate asked.

Lee stared at the two signs. He had no idea which one to choose. And doing *eany meany minie mo* in his head didn't help much; it simply made it even clearer that whichever option he chose would be a guess.

'The one on the right,' he said, not even daring to pronounce such long words in case he got them wrong.

As they turned into the new corridor Kate wondered out loud. 'Why don't they use normal words, like feet and heads and eyes?' she asked. 'Why do they have to use big long complicated ones that no-one understands?'

'Maybe the Mutants understand them,' Lee said. 'Maybe they're the only ones who understand them.'

'You mean ... ' Kate seemed taken aback by this new revelation. 'You mean the signs are in the Mutants' own language?'

Actually, that wasn't what Lee meant, but it was a really good idea – the sort of idea a leader could be expected to come up with – so he said 'Yes' anyway.

'No wonder we don't understand them! Wow, an alien language!'

'Ology probably means "for Mutants". Think about it. Radiology must mean Radios for Mutants. It's where they go if they want a radio with stations in their own language.'

'So what about gynaecology?' Kate asked.

'I don't know. Gynaecs must be something really technical that we haven't invented yet – something only the Mutants have.'

'Then they must have brought them from their own planet,' Kate said. 'Through the portal.'

'Quite possibly,' Lee agreed. 'Quite poss ... ' He stopped mid-sentence as the corridor widened into a more open area. 'Wait! Stop!' Lee whispered urgently. 'Look!'

'What?' Kate asked.

'What do you see?'

'Eh ... a lift?'

'Yes. But not just *any* old lift.'

'No?' Kate said, confused.

'This must be the one Will found. Remember, he said he found one that wasn't the main one. He said it must lead somewhere else.'

'Don't all lifts lead somewhere else?' Kate queried. 'Isn't that the point of them?'

'Well, yes, sort of. But if this is the one Will talked about, it must lead somewhere special. Maybe even to the portal!'

'Wow!'

They stopped and stared at it for a moment.

'I think we'd better keep looking around before we think

about getting into it,' Lee suggested. 'I still want to find that room Will talked about, the one with the ... '

Lee didn't finish his sentence because a ding suddenly came from the lift.

'Get us out of here!' he cried. 'That must be the alarm!'

Kate pushed as hard and as fast as she could manage.

'There must be someone coming out!' Lee whispered anxiously as they charged down the corridor. And then, seeing their chance of escape, called, 'Quick! In there!' as they came to a door. He stuck his foot out to push it open but the door didn't move.

'Oow!' Lee said as Kate backed up and he tugged at the door handle. It turned, and with a final shove they tumbled into the room.

'That was close,' Kate panted, trying to get her breath back.

'Too right,' Lee agreed, 'I thought we were going to get caught there.'

Lee was concentrating on rubbing his sore foot when Kate said, 'Look, Lee!'

He raised his head quickly, fearful they'd been spotted, but then sat open-mouthed. 'This must be it! This must be what Will was talking about!'

Yes, it had to be. All around the sides of the room arms

and legs were lying in piles. They had labels tagged to them, and at the other end of the room was a table on which an array of tools was laid out: spanners, screwdrivers, hammers and several tools Lee had never seen before.

'Amazing!' he said.

'I know, but what are we going to do about it?' Kate asked.

Lee already had a very good idea about what he wanted to do. However, now that he could see how many false limbs there were, he realised it was going to take more than the two of them.

'What time is it?' he asked. His own watch was still at home, and he hardly ever wore it anyway.

'Ten past twelve,' Kate told him.

'Right. We need to remember that?'

'Why?'

'Because whoever works here must go to lunch at this time.'

Kate nodded her understanding. 'We'd better not hang around here too long,' she said. 'What if they're a quick eater and come back soon.'

'You're right,' Lee said.

Kate moved towards the door. 'I'll check that the coast is clear.'

She had a good look, then turned and said, 'Okay, let's go.'

Lunch was about to be served as Kate wheeled Lee back into the ward. They arrived at his bedside at the same time as Isa was pushing the trolley along from the neighbouring bed.

'That was close,' Isa said.

For a second Lee thought she was talking about their narrow escape at the portal and wondered how she could possibly know about it, then he realised she meant he'd almost missed lunch.

'I didn't realise it was so late,' he told her. 'How time flies when you're enjoying yourself!'

'You must have smelled the food, eh? Is that what brought you back?'

What had actually brought them back had been the fear of being caught by Consul Mutants, transported through a portal and then forced to live the rest of their lives as slaves. But Lee didn't mention that. 'Well, the food you serve up always smells so good ... ' he said instead. Lee looked over to Kate and made a wiping motion over his brow as soon as Isa's head was turned.

'Lee, you can be a right little crawler sometimes,' Isa said. 'I'll tell you that for nothing.'

That was fine. It wasn't information Lee would have paid for anyway.

When lunch was over none of the nurses said anything, nor did any of the other kids. Only Andrew and Scott knew they'd gone. Now they were desperate to hear what Kate and Lee had discovered, and scurried over to Lee's bed even though it meant leaving some lunch on their plates.

'What happened?' Andrew pressed. 'Where did you go?'

'Did you find the portal?' Scott asked before Lee had a chance to answer Andrew's questions.

'Did you see any Mutants?' Andrew said, adding another question to the pile.

Lee held up his hands. He felt like an international superstar holding a press conference without any bodyguards to protect him from the thronging crowd. 'Woah! One question at a time,' he said. 'Don't mob me!'

Chapter Ten

Lee didn't sleep well, but when he awoke his body soon filled with a nervous energy. He stopped yawning every few minutes and started to become excited. It wouldn't be long before his plan would be put into action, and if it was successful he would save the whole of mankind from the Consul Mutants. Yes he was a little frightened, but he reminded himself that whatever risks they were about to take would be worth it to achieve such a momentous goal.

He sensed that Andrew and Scott hadn't slept well either. They were like soldiers before battle, thinking their private thoughts, not wanting to talk about the dangers that lay ahead until it was absolutely necessary. It was well into the morning before they came over to speak to him.

Scott arrived first, rolling across in his wheelchair and indicating the blanket Lee had instructed him to bring. 'It's roasting with this on me,' he complained.

'It's a small sacrifice,' Lee told him. 'This shouldn't take long, and I'll be bringing one, too.'

Scott didn't seem entirely heartened by the knowledge that they'd be experiencing the same level of discomfort.

Kate joined them, and moments later Andrew hopped over on his sticks.

'Right, are we all set?' Lee asked. 'Does everyone know where they're going and what to do when they get there?'

The other three nodded.

'Okay, Kate and I will go first. You follow on in a few minutes.'

Lee felt decisive – a real leader of men (and one girl). His moment of glory was drawing near and he wasn't going to shy away from it. He'd already thought up some titles for himself for when his name would be used in history books in years to come. *Lee The Great* seemed to be out of the question because some ancient king named Alfred had claimed the 'Great' title years ago. But *Lee The Mutant Mangler* sounded pretty good, he reckoned. As did *Lee The Alien Annihilator*. *Lee The Hospital Hero* wasn't quite so strong but would do for tabloid newspapers, whereas *Lee The All-Round Brilliant Guy* was a bit too general.

Scott and Andrew looked on as Kate pushed Lee's wheelchair down the centre of the ward.

'You don't think Scott and Andrew should have gone first?' Kate queried in a quiet voice. 'It'll take them quite a bit longer to get there with Andrew having to hop while he's pushing Scott's chair.'

'I don't think it'll matter. We should be able to do most of the work ourselves. If they're able to help towards the end then that'll be fine, but I don't think we need to worry about it.'

Kate shrugged. 'Okay, if you say so.'

They were a few steps from the ward doors when suddenly Nurse Chicken appeared in front of them. Lee would have jumped out of his chair if his legs had been strong enough. Instead, he jumped out of his skin.

'Sorry, Lee,' Nurse Chicken said, her wonderfully calming smile painted across her face. 'I didn't mean to scare you. What are you so jumpy about anyway?'

'Who? Me? Jumpy?'

'Well, you're not normally that easily startled.'

Credit where credit was due, Lee thought. At least she recognised that he usually had nerves of steel. It was just a pity those same nerves had turned to jelly when she'd stepped out in front of him.

Kate came to the rescue once again. 'Lee wants to go to the toilet.'

'That's right,' Lee chimed. 'I'm bursting for it.'

'Can you manage on your own?' Nurse Chicken asked.

'Well I'm not letting Kate help me,' he said. What a horrible thought! 'I've got a bit of strength back into my legs now, so I can manage once I'm there.'

'Well that's excellent! Good for you. It's great to see you trying so hard to get back on your feet again.' It took her a few seconds to realise she made a joke. 'Oh, back on your feet again!' She was laughing at her own humour, he realised, a sure sign of madness. Maybe the micro bugs the Mutants had planted in her brain weren't functioning quite as they were meant to.

'Well, I'll leave you two to it,' Nurse Chicken said. 'Better get on if you're bursting. We don't want any more accidents.'

Lee's face turned the colour of molten lava as Kate pushed him away from the embarrassment of Nurse Chicken's comments and, finally, out of the ward.

Would anyone notice them? Lee and Kate tried to stare straight ahead as they made their way along the same wide corridor they'd been down the day before, but it wasn't easy to resist watching other people to see if they were watching them back.

Where the corridor split they followed the arrows for Ophthalmology and Dermatology again.

Kate raised her head as they passed the door that the man in the white coat had come out of the last time. 'There are people in there!' she whispered to Lee, hurrying his wheelchair away in case anyone had seen her jumping up to get a look.

They stopped a little way back from the lift at which they'd almost been caught the previous day.

'Do you think the floor's alarmed?' Kate whispered.

Lee tried to work out why the floor would be alarmed. It had nothing to be scared of. He was about to say so when he realised what she meant. 'Oh yeah, it could be,' he said. 'We ought to be careful.'

Kate began tiptoeing across the open space in front of the lift doors, pushing Lee before her. They kept their eyes fixed on the panel alongside the lift, watching to see if it would ding and light up.

'Phew,' Kate whispered when they reached the other side without the alarm going off. She sped up down the short length of corridor until they were outside the room in which they'd discovered all the arms and legs. Next to the door was a sign they hadn't noticed before in their rush to get inside. *Prosthetics Maintenance*, it read. Neither of them knew what it meant, but that wasn't important. All that mattered was that they knew what to do next.

'What time is it?' Lee asked.

'You should wear a watch,' Kate scolded, looking at her own. 'How can you stick to precise military timing without one?'

'Yeah, yeah,' Lee said. 'We haven't got time for this.'

'How can you tell?' Kate said smugly.

'Alright, alright, I get the message,' Lee said impatiently. 'Let's get on with it.'

'It's eight minutes past twelve.'

'Right. Can you check to see if there's anyone in there?'

Kate stood at the side of the door and raised herself up until she could see through the small glass panel. There was a mesh of criss-crossing wires inside the glass to stop thieves putting their hands through if they broke the panel. It distorted Kate's view but she was still able to see that the room was empty.

'Excellent,' Lee said when she informed him that there was no-one around. He reached for the handle and turned it slowly. When it had gone as far as it could he said, 'Now here's hoping ... ' and pushed the door lightly.

It moved slightly inwards.

'We're in luck!' Lee whispered. 'It's as I thought. Whoever works here obviously never locks up when they go to lunch.'

With the door open a fraction, Lee peered in to make doubly sure no-one was about.

'All clear,' he told Kate and pushed the door fully open.

Kate quickly closed the door behind them. Lee removed the blanket that had been lying across his legs. He now knew what Scott meant about it being hot with it on. It was quite a relief to feel some cool air around his nether regions again.

'Right, let's get them stacked up,' he said, pointing to a bundle of false legs.

'They're creepy,' Kate said, holding back.

Lee knew it would have been better if he could have gone on this mission with another boy, someone who could be trusted not to get scared of stupid things like this. It was just the sort of girly cowardice he had feared might wreck his cunning plan. Right at the critical moment it seemed the arms and legs were going to be too much for Kate to handle.

But, despite her obvious misgivings, Kate did reach out and pick up a leg.

'Are they heavy?' Lee asked, impressed that Kate was getting on with what had to be done.

'A bit. Here ... ' She placed the leg carefully across Lee's chair.

'Hmm,' Lee said. 'It's not going to be very easy to hide them, is it. Not even with the blankets.'

He tried laying the leg so it pointed straight out, but that looked really stupid and obvious. Next he tried laying it diagonally. That was a little better, but not much. They couldn't go along corridors with the legs sticking out like that. So he tried laying it straight across his knees. It still stuck out at either side of the wheelchair, but he found that if he put the blanket back over his knees and leaned forward it didn't look too bad.

'It'll need to do,' Kate said. 'We don't have any other option.'

'You're right. Okay, give me another leg.'

Kate picked up another leg. 'At least the arms are shorter,' she observed. 'They'll be easier to disguise.'

They worked quickly, Kate passing Lee one leg after another. She was just passing him the final one when the door swung open.

Kate got such a fright that she dropped the leg she was holding. As it hit the ground it took a step on its own and Kate let out a scream. 'It's alive!' she cried, leaping away from it and seeking cover behind Lee's wheelchair.

It was Scott and Andrew who'd swung open the door, and now, together with Lee and Kate, they stared at the leg to see if it would move again.

It didn't.

'It must have been the way it landed,' Lee whispered. 'One

of the levers must have moved or something.'

'Man oh man,' Andrew said, spooked and clearly no longer relishing his task of loading arms on to Scott's lap.

'It's fine,' Lee said. 'Look!' He lifted up the blanket. Below it lay five legs, all motionless. 'See, it's perfectly alright. There's nothing to worry about.'

Gradually the others relaxed, even Kate.

'Now, can you close that door?' Lee asked, 'Or someone will realise we're in here.'

Andrew gave the door a gentle push, then started loading the false arms onto Scott's lap.

'This'll make life difficult for those ugly Consul Mutants!' Scott declared. 'They won't be able to get around Earth again in a hurry.'

Lee grinned. His plan was working. Will would be so impressed when he told him what they'd managed to do.

It didn't take long to get the arms on board, then Andrew and Kate pushed the two wheelchairs over to the door.

'Time?' Lee asked.

This time Kate didn't argue, though she did raise an eyebrow at him before she spoke.

'Twenty-five past twelve.'

'Come on. We'd better get a move on. Andrew, is it all clear outside?'

Andrew was taller than Kate, so it was easier for him to see through the glass.

'I think so … ' he was in the process of whispering when they all heard the sound of whistling coming up the corridor.

They squeezed in behind the door. Andrew and Kate crouching as low as they could, while Lee and Scott could only bend over in their wheelchairs.

Now it wasn't only whistling they could hear. There were footsteps, too, and each one was louder than the last. Would they pass or would they stop outside the door? In all the scary movies Lee had seen the footsteps kept on walking and the scared kids breathed a sigh of relief.

But this was no movie. This was real life. And so the footsteps stopped. Right outside the door.

The handle turned and they took a collective deep breath. The Consul Mutants were about to capture them. Soon they'd be on a one-way trip to the planet Skiv, and however much they were fascinated by space travel they didn't fancy experiencing it in the company of Imperial Consul Mutant Guards.

The whistling stopped and the door opened.

'Toilet,' they heard a male voice say. And then the door closed again.

None of them dared to breathe out until the footsteps and whistling started up again, and then became quieter as the man moved away.

'He's gone,' Kate eventually said, finally able to gulp a mouthful of fresh air.

'Yeah, but he'll soon be back,' Scott said. 'He's only going to the toilet.'

'Let's get out of here,' Andrew encouraged. Not that any of them needed any encouragement – the return of the Mutant had given them all the motivation they needed.

Andrew sneaked another look out of the window. This time it was all clear.

Kate opened the door and checked the corridor. It, too, was clear, so she wheeled Lee out. Andrew followed, hopping along behind Scott.

They crept along the corridor as quickly as they were able. Kate could move at full speed but Andrew had to stop every so often to rest his one good leg that was doing all the work.

There was no slowing down as they passed the lift this time. They pressed on until they reached the point where the corridor split. Kate stuck her head around the corner while she and Lee waited for Andrew and Scott to catch up. They were almost there. The storage cupboard where they would hide the artificial limbs was a short way along the corridor. Once they reached it they would be safe.

Kate looked back to Andrew and Scott and waved her arm impatiently, trying to get them to hurry up, then had another peek around the corner to make sure the corridor was still empty.

But it wasn't.

'Oh no!' she cried. 'It's him! He's coming this way!'

'Who?' Lee asked.

'Doctor Enleader! The Head Mutant! Oh no! The Whistler must have seen us after all and told Doctor Enleader what we were doing! We need to get out of here!'

Lee looked around, but realised they were trapped. They couldn't go back to the room because The Whistler would have told Doctor Enleader that was where he'd discovered them; and they couldn't press on because the evil Consul Mutant leader was blocking their way. In a few seconds he'd find out it was them who'd removed the artificial limbs. The game was up. There was no escape.

Chapter
Eleven

Or was there.

Because there was one option open to them if they dared to take it. It meant venturing into the unknown, but that had to be better than being caught by Mutants.

'Quick!' Lee instructed. 'The lift!'

Kate hesitated. 'What?'

'Get in!'

His order brought Kate to her senses. She spun Lee's wheelchair around and started running for the lift.

Andrew and Scott stopped in their tracks.

'What's happened?' Andrew asked urgently.

'Get into the lift!' Lee said. 'Doctor Enleader's coming!'

'Oh oh,' Scott said.

The lift was only a few metres behind them. Lee and Kate reached it first because they were already facing that way. Lee frantically pressed the call button, then stared at it, willing it to light up. 'Come on, come on,' Lee urged the lift. 'Hurry up.' Doctor Enleader would be round the corner any second, he knew, but still the light didn't come on, even though they could all hear the lift moving.

When they'd sped along the corridor the volume of their

pursuer's footsteps had decreased for a few moments as they'd put distance between themselves and him, but now they were ringing out clearly again, and were becoming louder still.

Then at last the lift dinged. They piled in as quickly as they could, thankful to find it empty. Andrew fell over in the rush and Kate had to help him up. Meanwhile, Lee pressed the only button he was able to reach from his wheelchair. It was marked with a 'B'.

The doors slid closed just as Doctor Enleader reached the lift. All Lee saw of him was a flash of white coat.

'Man, that was close,' Andrew said, rubbing his arm, which he'd banged in his fall.

However, they didn't have time to reflect on what had just happened because now they had to think about what might happen next.

'Where will this take us?' Scott asked anxiously.

As the doors began to slide open, Lee bent over in his chair, as much to protect his body against whatever lay outside the lift as to hide the artificial legs hidden under the blanket. Who knew what ravages lay at this level. He was beginning to wish his little sister were with him. She'd be a potent weapon, kicking and hitting anything in sight. And maybe because she was small and a girl the Mutants wouldn't fight back, just as his friends didn't, though Lee very much doubted that.

What if Andrew was right? What if the lift itself was the portal? Anything was possible after what they'd already experienced. Even that Andrew might for once be right.

The world that opened up before them was darker and eerier than the one they'd left behind in the hospital corridor. A complicated array of pipes and tanks stretched in front of them as far as they could see.

'What is that?' Scott whispered.

'I don't know,' Lee said without taking his eyes off the sight before them.

'No, not that,' Scott said, pointing ahead.

Lee turned round. 'What then?'

'That sound.'

They all listened hard.

Scott was right. There was a regular thumping sound coming from somewhere inside the complex.

'It's like a heartbeat,' Kate said. It was only after she'd uttered these words that their meaning became as clear to her as to the others.

'It must be the Queen Mutant!' Lee whispered. 'Just like

they have Queen Bees, this must be the Queen of the Consul Mutants!' He turned to Andrew. 'You were right! This *is* the portal, and the Queen is sitting right at the other end of it so the Mutants don't have too far to go to get to Earth. They must have a spaceship after all, and use it to get this far before crawling into the portal and then, at the other end, sliding into the room with the false limbs.'

'Could those tanks be where the Mutants live until they get their arms and legs?' Andrew asked, pointing into the middle of all the pipes before them.

'It would make sense,' Kate said. 'And then the Queen will have her own compartment somewhere else.'

'But what are we going to do now we're here?' Kate asked.

'Get straight back out again,' Scott said. 'I'm not hanging around here with the Queen. No way.'

'Okay. But first we need to hide these.' Lee raised the blanket on his legs then let it fall again. 'They're the key to stopping the Mutants getting about on Earth.'

Lee could see from Scott's terror-filled face that he wasn't keen on hanging around any more than was absolutely necessary. 'We'll do it as quickly as we can,' Lee said to reassure him.

Lee rolled his wheelchair forward and stuck his head

round the corner. There were no Mutants to be seen.

He faced Andrew and Scott. 'Right, you two stay here. Kate and I will try to find somewhere to hide these arms and legs. They'll never think of looking down here so close to their ship and their Queen. They'll assume the limbs will still be in the hospital.'

Scott and Andrew nodded, perfectly happy not to have to venture away from the portal.

'If we don't return,' Lee said, 'go back through the portal and tell someone who can try to rescue us.'

'Like who?' Scott asked.

'Like my Mum,' Kate said.

Lee wasn't convinced she'd be the best person. 'I don't know, but I'm sure you'll think of someone.'

'And we'd better wear these.' Lee reached up under his top and pulled out something he had, as part of his inspired plan, brought with him for just such a situation.

'What is it?' Scott asked with a puzzled look.

'It's material for anti-mind-control helmets.'

'Looks more like tin foil to me,' Andrew commented.

'It is. But what does tin foil do?'

Andrew and Scott stared blankly at each other.

'It reflects heat,' Kate stated.

'Exactly. And if it can reflect heat then it can also reflect the mutants' mind-control brainwaves.'

'Oh, right,' Scott said. 'It's a bit crinkly though, isn't it?'

'That's because it was around the baked potatoes I had for my dinner last night. Isa didn't notice I'd held it back. I've tried to flatten it out as best I can. Anyway, it will be better than nothing, because the mind-control waves will be incredibly strong down here, so close to their spaceship.'

With a few folds that an origami master would have been proud of, Lee transformed the crinkly foil into two hats. He handed one to Kate, who inspected it closely.

'Oh yuck! There's still some oil and potato skin on it. My hair will get all manky!'

Trust Kate to be worried about her hair when he had gone to great lengths to protect her from the threat of mind-control. 'Wash it later if you're that bothered,' Lee told her, sticking the remaining silver hat on his own head. It did feel a bit oily, but he put up with the discomfort. Kate made a face of displeasure as she gingerly placed her helmet on her head.

Lee tried to overcome everyone's nervousness with some decisive leadership. 'Come on. Let's go.'

Kate edged him out onto the concrete floor. Every movement they made seemed to be picked up by the spaceship and echoed back. Lee expected a Mutant sentry to jump out at any moment and drag them off to see the Queen, but by the time they'd travelled thirty or forty metres there was still no sign of Mutant life.

'Maybe they're all on Earth,' Lee said as quietly as possible. 'Maybe the spaceship is empty apart from the Queen.'

'Yeah, and she's too big to get out of it.'

'I hope so.'

Twenty metres further on they saw a door down a short dead-end. Lee pointed to it and Kate pushed him in its direction.

Unlike the hospital doors this one had no windows so they couldn't see what was on the other side.

'Shall we try it?' Kate asked.

'Might as well.' Lee reached out and gave the handle a tug. Nothing happened, so he tugged harder. Still nothing. 'It's locked,' he said. 'We'll need to find somewhere else.'

They backed up and followed the pipes along the corridor again. Soon they came to another dead-end, identical to the first one, including the door.

'Do you want to try this door?' Kate asked.

Lee nodded and they moved forward.

The wood was painted dark green, the colour of

pondweed, and the doorknob was covered in rust. Lee hesitated, not wanting to grab hold of it. But there was nothing else for it if he wanted to open the door, so he reached out and gave it a firm pull.

'Aw,' Lee said as it opened. Instead of leading to a secret passageway as he'd expected and hoped, it was simply a cupboard containing a couple of old spanners and a brush leaning against a small ladder at the back. It wasn't even very big.

But it was big enough for Lee's purpose. 'Perfect,' he declared. 'It looks as if they never use this place.'

He lifted the blanket and, with Kate's help, began unloading the artificial legs into the cupboard. The legs stacked easily in a corner, standing upright, one against the other like one-legged soldiers on parade.

Their task completed, they hurried back to the portal.

Andrew and Scott were extremely pleased to see them.

'The door keeps trying to close itself,' Andrew said. 'I've had to stand with my finger on this button the whole time you've been away.'

Lee was straight down to business. He didn't want to hang around a moment longer than was necessary.

'Right, Kate, you know where the cupboard is, so how about if you take Scott, and Andrew stays here with me to keep pushing the button?'

Lee removed his helmet and handed it to Scott, who inspected it briefly before reluctantly sticking it on his head.

Kate moved round to the back of Scott's wheelchair, even though it didn't seem the most appealing idea she'd ever heard.

'Quick as you can,' Lee said to them both as they made their way out of the portal.

Lee didn't know what was worse – creeping down the corridor to the storage cupboard or standing in the portal waiting for Kate and Scott to return. He felt so exposed with the door open. He was certain the Mutants must be able to see him standing there, yet no-one (or nothing) had shown itself.

There was a sudden bang and the portal started closing. Lee very nearly broke the world record for the high jump when he heard it.

Then the door opened again.

'Oops, sorry,' Andrew said. 'I took my finger off the button for a second. It was getting sore.'

Lee could hear his heart thumping in his chest, pounding like a bad headache. He hoped the others hadn't been too frightened by the noise. He listened carefully but heard nothing for the next minute.

Then suddenly, 'Ahhhh!' The cry came from where Kate and Scott would be. Andrew and Lee froze.

'Oh no! They've got them! Let's get out of here!' Andrew lifted his finger from the button and the doors started to close.

'No! Wait!' Lee told him. 'Open them again.'

Andrew did as he was instructed.

'We can't abandon them here,' Lee said.

He peered cautiously out of the portal. There was no sign of Scott and Kate heading back, but he could hear some sort of commotion and then was certain he heard Scott's voice.

'Did you hear that?'

'Yes.'

'Well, at least he's still alive.'

Another two minutes passed, then Lee saw Kate and Scott approaching in a hurry.

Kate bundled Scott's chair back in over the lip of the portal. Andrew immediately released his finger from the button and the portal slid closed.

'What happened?' Lee asked urgently, noticing that Scott and Kate had both lost their helmets. 'What was all that noise about?'

'This!' Scott said, lifting the blanket from over his legs to reveal an artificial arm still underneath.

'How come ...?'

Kate explained. 'When we were moving them we must have hit this one's controls because it suddenly grabbed hold of the side of Scott's wheelchair.'

'Yeah, and it won't let go!' Scott added. 'We've tried everything.'

'But we can't take it back with us,' Lee told them. 'If they see it they'll know it was us!'

'We don't have any choice,' Kate said. 'Not unless you know how to release the grip of the hand.'

It was like a bad comedy, Lee thought. He could picture a gang of criminals breaking into a bank only to find the money covered in glue so all the police needed to do was find people with money stuck to their fingers. The situation they were now in bore another similarity to a bad comedy: no-one was laughing.

Lee felt they ought to be celebrating, but as well as the unexpected problem of the hand that wouldn't let go of Scott's wheelchair, they still had to get back through the portal and into the ward, and he was worried that by now someone would have noticed their prolonged absence.

'We'll need to think about it on our way back,' Lee said,

not wanting to hang around any longer. He motioned to Andrew to send the portal on its way.

There were only two buttons, so Andrew pressed the one he hadn't been pressing a few seconds ago.

The portal started moving and Lee could feel himself passing between worlds, from one planet to another. He wrestled with the arm that was grasping the wheelchair but it was locked on.

'What now?' Scott asked as the lift shuddered to a halt again.

'We'll need to go back separately,' Lee said.

'Well that's okay,' Andrew told him, 'because Kate can walk faster than me anyway. So you'll get back ahead of us.'

'But what about this?' Scott asked, pointing to the arm that didn't want to let go.

'Cover it up with your blanket.'

'But what about when I get back? Someone's bound to see it.'

'Not if you keep your blanket over it all the time.'

The doors opened. Again they looked out nervously.

'We've made it!' Lee announced. 'We're back on Earth.'

Their excitement was blunted by the knowledge that they were only a few metres beyond the room they'd originally taken the arms and legs from. Doctor Enleader could still be there.

The doors started closing because they'd hesitated too long and Andrew urgently reached for the button. He had no intention of being transported back through the portal again, not having just left behind the Mutant Queen and her spaceship.

'Right, see you back in the ward,' Lee said and Kate began pushing his chair as fast as she could manage, leaving Scott and Andrew to follow on behind.

'Where have you two been?' Nurse Chicken asked, her face serious. 'We've been worried about you.'

'We took a wrong turn and got lost,' Lee said.

'Sorry,' Kate added.

'You haven't seen Scott and Andrew on your travels, have you?'

'Eh ... no,' Lee said, as if he could hardly remember who Scott and Andrew were.

'Well next time you need the toilet make sure you go straight there and back.'

'Will do,' Kate said. Then, to distract Nurse Chicken, she asked, 'Ehm, have you seen Doctor Donald?'

Nurse Chicken's face instantly brightened as a picture of the handsome doctor flooded into her mind. 'I ... ehm ... Not in the last hour,' she said, all flustered. 'He's probably on his lunch break.'

Lunch! In all the excitement Lee had forgotten to be hungry. Now his stomach was reminding him with a series of thunderous rumbles.

'Has Isa been round already?' he asked.

'I'm afraid so.'

Lee tried his saddest face on her, turning down the sides of his mouth so far that someone could easily have tripped over them.

It worked.

'Okay, I'll ask Isa if she can microwave you some of whatever's left in the kitchen.'

'Thanks!' Lee and Kate told her together.

As Kate started pushing Lee towards his bed Nurse Chicken exclaimed again. 'You two!' Lee and Kate swivelled round, thinking she was calling after them, but it was Scott and Andrew she was about to interrogate.

'I hope they keep their mouths closed and that arm covered,' Lee said as they reached his bed. He felt tired again, the way he had during those first few days in hospital, but this time he knew it was the stress of leadership and success that was causing it. That and lack of food.

HOSPITAL PATIENTS ARE HOPPING MAD

A group of patients at Royal General Hospital are said to be outraged after their artificial arms and legs were apparently stolen.

The bizarre robbery took place around midday on Thursday. Several patients had deposited their limbs with the Prosthetics Department for routine maintenance, such as oiling, but when the maintenance technician returned from lunch the limbs were found to be missing. In total, six patients are without legs and five are without arms.

Police are baffled. They say they can't imagine what the thieves could use the arms and legs for.

'It's as if aliens have dropped out of the sky and mistaken them for something else,' PC David Copper told this paper.

Consultant Doctor Ali Enleader, head of the Prosthetics Department said, 'Perhaps it seems like a joke to whoever's taken these arms and legs, but it is making life extremely difficult for those who're now without them, and I would appeal to the thieves or pranksters to return them immediately.'

Lee's dad began laughing as Lee read the end of the story in the newspaper clipping he'd been handed.

'It's funny, isn't it! I thought it might bring a smile to your face, that's why I brought it in for you.'

Lee tried very hard to magic up the sort of big, broad grin he imagined his dad was thinking of, but knew he wasn't being in the least bit convincing.

'But Doctor Enleader ...' Lee said, letting his smile slip. 'He's a Mutant.' Lee didn't expect his dad to understand. All adult humans, it seemed, were under the power of the Mutants, but he had to try to explain what was going on.

'A Mutant?' Lee's dad said, chortling. He stared at Doctor Enleader's picture in the newspaper. 'I wouldn't say he's *that* ugly.'

'No, Dad, you don't understand! I'm serious! He's a Consul Mutant!'

Lee's dad burst out laughing. 'A Consul Mutant. That's clever, that is. That's really clever. Consultant – Consul Mutant!'

'What ...?' Lee asked, confused. 'What's a consultant?'

'A senior doctor,' his dad said. 'A specialist in a particular area of medicine.' He still seemed to be finding something funny in what Lee had said. 'When did you come up with that one, eh?'

Lee looked around for a means of escape. Escape from the ward; escape from Scott and Andrew and Kate; escape from the staff; but mainly escape from the humiliating embarrassment he now felt.

What had he done? How had he managed to mix up Consultants with Consul Mutants? Had his hearing been altered by all the drugs the nurses and doctors had been pumping into him? Or had his brain been warped? He was normally a rational, intelligent boy, not the sort of idiot who would easily confuse two words and deduce that the world was being taken over by life-forms from another planet. There had to be some other explanation.

Lee wanted to disappear under his bedcovers, to hide in the darkness there and pretend, once again, that he was asleep. Maybe then he could wake up and find it had all been a dream, just like people did in totally unconvincing TV programmes.

But this wasn't a dream. It wasn't even a hideously creepy nightmare. It was reality. And his dad was there to prove it, as was Scott's wheelchair at the other side of the ward, still complete with the false arm.

Everyone was going to laugh at him for being so stupid. *Loony Lee* they would probably call him. There would be no posters of him on every bedroom and classroom wall providing inspiration for millions across the country. And there would be no invitations onto TV chat shows, or lucrative sponsorship deals, or any of the other trappings of success. He would need to leave home and live in a cold, dark, damp cave on a deserted island, far away from the rest of humanity, living off fish he would have to catch and kill with his own bare hands. And he didn't even like fish.

It wasn't a future he was looking forward to.

But then Lee remembered. *He* hadn't mixed up consultants with consul mutants; it was Kate who'd first told him about the Mutants. It was *her* fault.

Well wasn't that just typical of a girl? Couldn't they get *anything* right? Look at all the trouble her mistake had caused!

'Oh well,' his dad said, 'I've no doubt they'll turn up somewhere. It's probably just someone having a bit of 'armless fun, eh?' He nudged Lee, his usual way of indicating he'd made a joke.

Lee cringed, as he often did at his dad's jokes, but then they were usually dreadful.

'Don't you think it's funny?' his dad asked.

No, Lee didn't think it was funny. He might have done if he'd had nothing to do with the missing arms and legs, but he'd masterminded their disappearance! He had an image in his head of a room in which six patients were hopping around, each on their one remaining good leg, waiting for the return of their artificial one. In this vision the one-legged patients fell over every so often because they couldn't keep their balance. Lee felt terrible about it. And when he looked up the ward to where Scott sat it was impossible for his eyes not to be drawn to the wheelchair at the side of the bed, the blanket still covering the arm that wouldn't let go.

What a mess he'd made. How could he put it right?

'Are you okay?' his dad asked.

'Eh, yeah. Fine. I'm just a bit tired, Dad.'

'Okay. Well I'll head off then and let you get some sleep, shall I?'

'Maybe that would be best,' Lee said, though he knew only too well that he wouldn't be able to sleep until he'd figured out a way to clear up the mess he'd created.

The solution popped into Lee's head at five past ten that evening, by which time he'd been thinking about it for a full two hours.

His new plan was brilliant and inspired. Inspired, that was, by the need to get himself and the others out of trouble before anyone discovered the arm attached to Scott's wheelchair.

However, he would have to wait until the next morning before he could put his latest plan into action.

The next day was a Saturday and Lee knew that his mum was coming in to see him that morning. More importantly (at least for his new plan), Lee knew Will would be coming with her.

But before all that there were other events to occupy his time. First, there was the arrival of breakfast, courtesy of wrinkly crinkly Isa, who still hadn't ironed her skin.

'I'sa got the usual feast for you,' she joked. 'Extra large bowl is it?'

But Lee wasn't very hungry. For once he had more important things on his mind than food. 'Just a small one,' he informed Isa, who raised her eyebrows in surprise.

Then, after he'd eaten, Nurse Chicken insisted he have a wash. 'You don't want to be all stinky and smelly when your mum gets here, do you,' she said.

Lee wasn't aware that he was stinky or smelly. 'I don't think I need a wash,' he told her.

'Ah, but pigs can't smell their own muck,' she told him.

This struck Lee as being the sort of argument you could never win. If you could smell yourself then you needed a wash, whereas if you couldn't smell yourself ... well, apparently you still needed a wash. In that case, Lee decided, everyone in the world needed a wash all of the time, so it was amazing there was ever a bathroom free anywhere on the planet.

Having refreshed himself, Lee returned to his bed. Instead of sitting in it he sat beside it, as he was now able to do. Strengthening his legs was taking a while, but he could now stand on his own okay and manage a few paces along the side of the bed – even if he did have to cling to the frame for support.

At first Lee had thought he would have to tell the others about his – or rather Kate's – mix up between the Consultants and Consul Mutants. There didn't seem to be any way out of it. He would have to accept losing his credibility on the ward and go back to being the old Lee – the Lee that no-one noticed or respected – even though that was something he really didn't want, because he liked being respected by the others and enjoyed being the leader for once instead of being overlooked.

However, he now thought it might be possible to retain that respect. With his new plan there could be a way of putting everything right on his own so that none of the others would have to know that their adventures, hard work and fear had been unnecessary. It would require immaculate timing and a bit of luck, but it could be done.

So it was with great relief that Lee saw his mum and Will enter the doors of the ward. As they approached, Lee could see his mother was carrying another envelope. He presumed it was a further batch of Get Well Soon cards from his classmates. Oh joy. After the last bundle he hardly dared think about the warm-hearted messages this lot might contain.

'Hi there, Putchkin Darling,' his mum greeted him in her usual embarrassing voice.

Will gave Lee a shrug and a look of despair, which together Lee took to mean, 'She's *your* mum, can't you do something about her?' or, 'I'd be so embarrassed if my mum called me those stupid names,' or perhaps it was simply, 'This woman is totally bonkers!'

'Look, more cards from your classmates!' his mum enthused. 'Isn't that kind of them? They're obviously all still missing you. Mind you, not for much longer.'

'No?' Lee queried.

'That's right, Lamb Chops. The Consultant says you

should be able to go home in three days time! Isn't that great?'

'Eh ... yeah. Will I have to go straight back to school.'

Will gave Lee another look. This one said, 'Nice try, Lee.'

'Of course,' his mum told him. 'I'll bet you can't wait to get back.'

'Yeah, that's right. Believe me, there's nothing I'd rather do.'

'Oh come on, it won't be that bad.'

Lee was just persuading himself that she was probably right when a thought struck him. 'Mum, what if I can't walk properly by then?'

'You can take your wheelchair with you,' she said. 'The consultant's already said that's okay.'

'But Mum ... ' Lee was thinking of what it would be like to arrive at school in a wheelchair. Everyone would laugh at him. He'd be the butt of every joke.

So he was surprised to hear Will say, 'Wow, cool!'

'Why's it cool?' Lee asked him.

'You'll be first in the queue at lunchtime. For once someone might get in before Angelina Bottle!'

'And you could come with me!' Lee suddenly realised.

'Oh yeah, I hadn't thought of that,' Will said in a voice that meant he clearly had thought about it.

'No doubt everyone will want to know the gory details of your operations,' his Mum said. 'But I suppose that's kids for you.'

Actually, that didn't sound too bad either, Lee thought. He might even be able to show them his scars. That would be cooler than a freezer!

And, of course, if his plan worked out no-one at school would need to know that Consul Mutants weren't really dangerous aliens from outer space.

Suddenly going back to school didn't seem such a bad prospect after all. He began to see his return as that of a conquering hero. 'Hail Lee, survivor of the deadly appendix disease and only person in the class to have spent several weeks in hospital,' they might call upon his arrival. 'And hail as well for being incredibly brave in the face of terrifying Mutants, and especially for evading their mind-control techniques in order to save the world from a terrible fate.'

And maybe The Ogre would have to be nice to him for a change ...

Yes, it was all starting to sound much more promising.

'It's got to be more fun than lying around here,' Will said.

'Actually, this place isn't so bad,' Lee said, surprising himself. 'It can be quite good fun sometimes.'

'You've made a few friends, haven't you,' his mum said.

Lee nodded and reached for the cards.

Dear Leah,
I didn't notice you weren't at skool, except
The Ogre said I had to make you a card,
butt git well soon anyway.
From Simon

Simon's spelling was just as bad as Craig's. However, Lee suspected 'butt' and 'git' were deliberate.

Dear Squirt,
Making cards is better than Maths, so stay in hospital for
ages so we can make some more.
From David

Dear Lie,
When my gran died it cost a lot for the coffin.
So try to stay alive so you can use your pocket
money for sweets instead.
From Jack

Dear Lee,
Hurry up and get well again.

That was more like it. Lee looked to see whose name was at the bottom of the card. It was Will's. Even though he was in another class, The Ogre must have asked if he'd wanted to include a card, knowing they were best friends. Lee supposed that was actually quite decent of her.

'Thanks, Will,' Lee said. 'That's the best card I've had.'

'No problem,' Will told him, pleased but not realising how limited the competition was. 'And guess what?'

'What?'

'It's good news.'

'What is!'

'We're not moving house after all!'

'That's fantastic!' Lee almost leapt out of his bed with joy but bounced up and down instead.

'We're getting an extension built, so no need.'

Lee was over the moon and, since things were going so well, decided this was the perfect time to put his latest plan into action. 'Eh, Mum, could I get my comic to read, for after you've gone?'

'Sure, Honey Pie. Perhaps Will would like to go to the shop and get it for you?' she suggested.

'Eh, well I haven't seen him for quite a while ... '

'Oh, I see. You boys want some time to yourselves to catch up on the gossip, do you?'

She made them sound like a couple of old biddies meeting in the street:

'Did you see Mrs Smith at number 23 has got a new cat?'

'Oh really? What happened to her old one?'

'She gave it a bath, then tried to dry it in the microwave.'

'Oh dear, poor moggy.'

'It was terrible. Cooked it from the inside out.'

'But at least it's dry?'

'Oh yes. And she never lets anything go to waste. She uses its skin as a hand towel for visitors.'

Despite this unwelcome image of himself and Will, Lee managed to raise a smile for his mother.

'Okay, I'll go and get it for you. I'll grab a coffee at the same time. I didn't have one before I came out.' She gathered up her handbag. 'You'll be fine here, won't you Will?'

Will said he would be and Lee's mum headed off.

'What was that all about?' Will asked as soon as she was out of earshot.

'Quick, we don't have long,' Lee said, looking over to where Scott was sitting, guarding the wheelchair next to him that still had the blanket draped over it.

Lee stood up and managed to stagger the few steps to his own wheelchair.

'Will, can you push me?'

'Eh, sure. But where are we going? And what's the rush?'

'I'll explain on the way,' Lee told him. 'Right, take me to Scott's bed first.'

It only took a few seconds for them to cross the ward. Once there, Lee explained to Scott as much of the plan as he felt he had to, all the while keeping an eye out for doctors and nurses.

'You want to swap chairs?' Scott said, confused.

'Yes,' Lee said.

'Eh, well, if you want to. You know this one's still got ... '

'Yes, yes, I know. That's *why* I want it. I'm going to get rid of it.'

'Well if you're sure ... '

Lee didn't wait a second longer. After another check to ensure no-one could see him he stood again and shuffled into Scott's wheelchair.

'We'll leave mine,' he told Will, who by now was totally baffled as to what was going on. 'Right, we need to get out of here.'

Despite not knowing what part he was playing, Will began pushing Lee down the corridor.

As they reached the ward doors Nurse Chicken appeared, as if she were the ward's sentry.

'Where are you off to *this* time?' she asked.

'The toilet again,' Lee said.

'*Again?* Right. Well you won't get lost like last time, will you?'

'No. I promise. I know exactly where it is now.'

'Okay,' Nurse Chicken said doubtfully. 'Well I'll expect to see you back here in a couple of minutes, shall I?'

Lee had to nod and Nurse Chicken moved out of their path.

'We'll need to be extra quick,' Lee said to Will as soon as she was out of earshot.

'I don't even know what we're doing!' Will said. 'I might be able to help if you tell me.'

'We need to find another wheelchair,' Lee told him.

'But why? You've already got one. How are you going to sit in two at the same time?'

'No, no. I don't want two, I just want to swap them round.'

'But why? What's wrong with this one?'

The part of the corridor they were in was empty. 'Right, stop a second,' Lee said. Then, beckoning Will close to him he lifted up the blanket so Will could see beneath it.

Will caught sight of four fingers and a thumb grasping the side of the wheelchair and knew instantly that they weren't from Lee's hand.

'Aaggghhh ...!!!' he hollered, and began running back down the corridor towards the ward.

'Will!' Lee shouted after him. 'Come back! It's alright!'

Will slowed and then stopped but showed no sign of wanting to return to where Lee was sitting, stranded. Lee waved his arm urgently and then, in desperation, lifted the end of the arm that wasn't attached to the wheelchair so that Will could see it. 'It's not a real one,' he whispered loudly.

It was the appearance of a nurse behind him that persuaded Will to rejoin Lee, who had to hurriedly cover the arm with the blanket before the nurse saw it.

'Man, you gave me a fright,' Will said as he drew nearer. 'You should have told me!'

'I couldn't, there wasn't time.'

'What are you going to do with it?'

'It won't come off. That's why I need to get a new chair ... ' Lee let his voice trail off. 'Like that one, there!' he said, pointing at a wheelchair that was sitting outside a door at the end of the corridor. 'Perfect!'

'But whoever it belongs to is going to find that ... that thing, that arm on their chair.'

'That can't be helped,' Lee said. 'Needs must be.'

Will let out a long sigh and didn't say anything.

'Let's get on with it. We have to get back before Nurse Chicken sends out a search party. We can't get caught with this arm on us.'

'And before we bump into your mum,' Will added, realising the tricky position they were in.

'Exactly. So let's get on with it.'

Will began pushing again. Reaching the end of the corridor they were relieved to discover that the abandoned wheelchair was identical to Scott's.

'Standard issue,' Lee said. 'I think they must all be exactly the same.'

They heard voices on the other side of the door they were standing outside.

'Quick!' Will said, and Lee raised himself out of one chair and into the other. Will was about to start pushing again when Lee whispered, 'Wait!' He took a piece of paper from his pocket and dropped it onto the seat of the wheelchair with the arm. 'Go, go!' he then urged.

Will pushed as if racing for the line in a sprint, so fast, in fact, that Lee began to wonder if it would be a good idea for wheelchairs to be supplied with air bags in case of high-speed crashes.

Behind them they heard the door open. 'Oh,' a woman's voice said. 'Look, someone must've dropped their blanket on your ... '

Lee and Will were rounding the corner of the corridor when they heard the scream. It chased after them like a banshee.

Will ran even more quickly until they reached the ward door.

'Well done,' Lee said. 'Though I was worried we might get stopped by the police. We must have been doing over thirty miles an hour.'

'Just as well there weren't any speed cameras,' Will panted. He took a few more deep breaths then said, 'What did that note say?'

'What note?'

'The one you left on the chair.'

'Oh, that note. It was a warning to the Mutants not to mess with us.'

'Good idea,' Will said. 'That'll tell them who's boss.'

What the note actually told *them* – the hospital staff – was where to find all the other arms and legs. To ensure his handwriting didn't give him away, Lee had 'written' his note using letters cut out from newspaper headlines. It had taken an age to stick all the letters on a separate sheet, but it had been worth it to preserve his anonymity and reputation.

Chapter
Thirteen

(Unlucky for Consul Mutants)

'Right, young man,' Doctor Donald said. 'I think it's about time we got rid of you.'

Beside him, Nurse Chicken beamed. Lee knew it was more because she was next to Doctor Donald than because she was glad to see the back of him. At least, he hoped that was the case.

'You'll need to take things easy for a few weeks,' Doctor Donald said, 'but there's no reason why you can't go home later this morning.'

Isa joined them at his bedside and must have overheard Doctor Donald. 'It'll be a shame not to see you around,' she said, handing him a bowl of cereal. 'But I'sa pleased you're better now.'

Lee grinned. He loved people who could laugh at themselves. He would miss Isa. More to the point, he'd miss having breakfast served up to him in bed every day.

At that moment Doctor Enleader, the tall man in the white coat, the one Lee had seen on the first day and had thought was one of the Mutants' leaders, walked up the centre of the ward, head held high.

Doctor Enleader seemed to be heading for Scott's bed.

Lee tried to conceal his panic. He was sure they had been rumbled. Doctor Enleader was going to confront Scott and force him to tell everything.

Whatever Lee's concerns at that moment, Nurse Chicken seemed to be finding something very amusing.

'What is it?' Lee asked nervously.

'Oh, you should see your face,' Nurse Chicken said through the laughter that threatened to fold her in two as she backed away from Lee's bed. 'But you needn't worry, your secret's safe with me.'

Lee was confused for all of five seconds. Then all doubts about returning home evaporated. He wanted out as soon as possible.

But there were goodbyes to be said before he could say good riddance.

Kate actually left hospital before him, the new valve in her heart having been given the 'all clear'. To Lee's way of thinking, if it had managed to withstand the shocks of the last few days it had to be working perfectly.

She told Lee, Scott and Andrew that she'd had a great time, even though she'd had to hang around with a bunch of boys. For their part, the boys said she'd been okay, too.

For a girl, anyway.

Scott was to be allowed out the day after Lee, whereas Andrew would have to wait a few days longer. Lee shook their hands as he headed for the double doors of the ward for the last time. 'Hopefully I won't see you soon,' Scott said, 'otherwise it'll mean we're all ill again! But here's my address and telephone number.' He handed a piece of paper to Lee. 'Give me a call if there's any more Mutant bashing to be done.'

Lee grinned. 'You never know where they're going to pop up next, do you,' he said.

'Good morning, everyone.'

'Good morning, Mrs Ogre,' all the boys replied, as ever leaving the girls to cover for them by saying her name properly.

'And a very special good morning to Lee,' she said, 'who's back with us after a few weeks in hospital. Lee, we all hope you're feeling much better and are raring to get stuck into catching up with your work, yes?'

'I'm certainly feeling better now, thanks,' Lee said.

'Well,' The Ogre carried on, 'I'm sure everyone must be very keen to hear all that happened when you were in hospital.'

'Well it'll be in my book,' Lee said.

The Ogre seemed amused at the idea. 'Oh right, you're thinking of writing a book about it? Well, we'll all look forward to that, won't we class!'

Lee's classmates sniggered.

How dare they, Lee thought. He decided right there and then that he would write a book about his adventures, though obviously he wouldn't use his real name on the cover.

'Can I just say, uhm, thanks for all the, ehm, cards I received.'

'Oh good, I'm glad you liked them,' The Ogre said.

'Eh, yes. They were very humourless.'

'Humorous,' The Ogre corrected him.

But Lee just grinned at the rest of the class.

THE END

(for real this time!)

Your Thoughts

If you have any thoughts about this book, or if you simply want to complain about the jokes in it, please contact Keith via his website:

www.keithcharters.co.uk

where you can also get details on more books in the Lee series.

Meeting his dad's multizillionaire boss inspires Lee to come up with a get-rich-quick scheme of his own.

But not everyone is keen for Lee to succeed. Local shopkeeper Panface isn't, and it seems that he has sneaky spies out there, trying to ruin Lee's plans.

Will Lee get the better of his rivals? Or will he spend the whole time daydreaming about how many houses he'll own and how many butlers he'll have?

Lee will need to rely on his common sense and financial genius if he's to succeed in business ... so it could be a struggle.

Lee Goes For Gold
Keith Charters
ISBN 978-1-905537-25-9
(paperback, RRP £6.99)

Nothing is ever straightforward when Lee is around...not even a summer holiday in Spain.

It ought to be a case of lazing by the pool, but Lee is soon spying on dodgy men in shiny suits and sunglasses, battling with a family that seems determined to ruin everyone's holiday and haranguing horrendous holiday reps.

With so much going on, how will Lee ever get a tan?

Lee's Holiday Showdown
Keith Charters
ISBN 978-1-905537-26-6
(paperback, RRP £6.99)

Lee has won the chance to be The First Child In Space. It's amazing what you can win these days by filling in a form on the back of a cereal packet!

Under the command of Captain Slogg, and with Sports Bob at the controls, Lee blasts off for the Moon on the trip of a lifetime. However, he and his fellow astronauts are not the only ones with their eyes on the big lump of cheese in the sky.

When disaster strikes, Lee faces the most important challenge of his life. If he succeeds he will return to Earth a hero. If he fails, he may not return at all.

Lee on the Dark Side of the Moon
Keith Charters
ISBN 978-1-905537-13-6
(paperback, RRP £6.99)

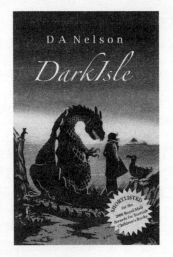

For 10-year-old Morag, there's nothing magical about the cellar of her cruel foster parents' home. But that's where she meets Aldiss, a talking rat, and his resourceful companion, Bertie the dodo. She jumps at the chance to run away and join them on their race against time to save their homeland from the evil warlock Devlish, who is intent on destroying it. But first, Bertie and Aldiss will need to stop bickering long enough to free the only guide who knows where to find Devlish: Shona, a dragon who's been turned to stone.

Together, these four friends begin their journey to a mysterious dark island beyond the horizon, where danger and glory await—along with clues to the disappearance of Morag's parents, whose destiny seems somehow linked to her own ...

DarkIsle
D A Nelson
ISBN 978-1-905537-04-4
(paperback, RRP £6.99)